And then there was Au

She was the only woman he'd never forgotten.

The one regret that kept him up at night. Not only was she here in Royal, but she was staying right next door and using his pool wearing a scrap of fabric for a bikini.

Yep. Either he was being punked or the universe was having a nice laugh at his expense.

A light went on upstairs in the house next door, and his eyes were automatically drawn there.

Audra.

Probably preparing a bubble bath with her drink in hand.

Darius shut his eyes against the erotic image that suddenly flooded his brain, his body stiffening in response.

There would be a lot of cold showers and sleepless nights in his future.

* * *

Secret Heir Seduction by Reese Ryan is part of the Texas Cattleman's Club: Inheritance series.

Dear Reader,

Family can be complicated and messy. Add secrets and lies to the mix, and it's like lighting the fuse on a powder keg. No one knows that better than Darius Taylor-Pratt.

In *Secret Heir Seduction*, the fashion designer comes to Royal to pursue the opportunity of a lifetime. What he gets instead is the deceased father he never knew, siblings he never asked for and an encounter with the ex he walked away from five years ago. Gorgeous diamond heiress and jewelry designer to the stars Audra Lee Covington is temporarily living in Royal, away from her most recent ex, a handsome politician who is still campaigning for her heart.

Neither Darius nor Audra wish to revisit the past. But fate has other plans.

Thank you for reading this installment of Texas Cattleman's Club: Inheritance! Be sure to read the complete series.

To discover my Bourbon Brothers and Pleasure Cove series, visit reeseryan.com/desirereaders. For series news, reader giveaways and more, join my VIP Readers newsletter list and private reader Facebook group.

Until our next adventure,

Reese Ryan

REESE RYAN

SECRET HEIR SEDUCTION

HARLEQUIN

DESIRE

Special thanks and acknowledgment are
given to Reese Ryan for her contribution to the
Texas Cattleman's Club: Inheritance miniseries.

Recycling programs
for this product may
not exist in your area.

ISBN-13: 978-1-335-20895-8

Secret Heir Seduction

Copyright © 2020 by Harlequin Books S.A.

For questions and comments about the quality of this book,
please contact us at CustomerService@Harlequin.com.

Harlequin Enterprises ULC
22 Adelaide St. West, 40th Floor
Toronto, Ontario M5H 4E3, Canada
www.Harlequin.com

Printed in U.S.A.

Reese Ryan writes sexy, emotional romance with captivating family drama, surprising secrets and a posse of complex characters.

A Midwesterner with deep Southern roots, Reese currently resides in semi-small-town North Carolina, where she's an avid reader, a music junkie and a self-declared connoisseur of cheesy grits. Reese is the author of the Bourbon Brothers and Pleasure Cove series.

Connect with her via Instagram, Facebook, Twitter or at reeseryan.com.

Join her VIP Readers Lounge at bit.ly/VIPReadersLounge.

Books by Reese Ryan

Harlequin Desire

The Bourbon Brothers

Savannah's Secret
The Billionaire's Legacy
Engaging the Enemy

Dynasties: Secrets of the A-List

Seduced by Second Chances

Texas Cattleman's Club: Inheritance

Secret Heir Seduction

Visit her Author Profile page at Harlequin.com, or reeseryan.com, for more titles.

You can find Reese Ryan on Facebook, along with other Harlequin Desire authors, at Facebook.com/harlequindesireauthors!

To the amazing readers who read and recommend my books, especially the members of the Reese Ryan VIP Readers Lounge, y'all rock. I'm grateful you've chosen to come along for the ride.

To Kristan Higgins, LaQuette, Megan Frampton, Robin Covington, Lauren Dane, Cheris Hodges, Michelle Styles, Piper Huguley, Patricia W. Fischer, Naima Simone, HelenKay Dimon and all of my fellow authors who've read and shared my books... thank you from the bottom of my heart for your kindness and generosity.

One

Darius Taylor-Pratt sat in front of a heavy mahogany desk and surveyed the space around him.

The room's dark decor seemed better suited to an older man than to upbeat lifestyle guru and reality TV star Miranda Dupree.

Miranda, founder of the Goddess health and lifestyle brand, had invited him to Royal, Texas, for a meeting. She'd proposed a collaboration with Thr3d, his quickly growing performance wear company, to create a Goddess-branded line of athletic wear.

The timing was terrible.

His team was preparing for their first LA Fashion Week runway show. Still, this deal could catapult Thr3d to the next level. So he hadn't been able to board the plane she'd sent for him quickly enough.

Heavy footsteps approached. Too heavy to be the

five-foot-three, redheaded sprite. Miranda probably weighed less than a buck twenty-five.

A man with a messy shock of brown hair, brown eyes and a five o'clock shadow entered the room.

"Hello, Darius. I'm Kace LeBlanc." The man extended his hand. "Attorney."

Darius regarded him warily as he stood to shake his hand. "Don't lawyers typically get involved *after* an agreement has been reached?"

Kace thumbed through papers in a folder already on the desk. "In a business deal, yes. But I'm not Miranda's lawyer."

"Then whose attorney are you, Mr. LeBlanc?" Darius's shoulders tensed.

"I represent the estate of Mr. Buckley Blackwood, recently deceased. The estate which he left to his ex-wife, Miranda Dupree Blackwood."

"How nice for her."

That explains the furniture, but not why he's here.

Darius returned to his seat and glanced at his black-and-gold Tissot chronograph watch before meeting the man's gaze again. "Will it be much longer before Miranda joins us?"

"I apologize for the subterfuge in bringing you here. But you've been summoned to meet with me about a completely different matter."

"Miranda has no interest in partnering with my company?" When the man didn't respond, Darius shot to his feet. "Look, I don't know what this is about, but I'm a busy man. I don't have time for your little shell game."

"I assure you, you'll want to hear what I have to say," the man said calmly. "I only need ten minutes of your time. When I'm done, if you'd still like to head straight back to LA, the driver will take you to a fueled and ready plane."

Darius set his stopwatch. "You've got exactly ten minutes." He sank onto the chair. "Why am I here?"

"Does the name Buckley Blackwood mean anything to you?"

Darius shrugged. "I know he's Miranda's ex-husband, and that he owned a bank."

"Plus this six-hundred-acre ranch, homes around the globe and investments in a variety of other business interests, like Thr3d."

"You're saying he invested in my company?" *Impossible.* He knew the names of every investor. Buckley Blackwood wasn't one of them.

"He invested in Thr3d using a shell company."

"That still doesn't explain why I'm here." Darius's patience was wearing thin.

"You're here for a private reading of Buck's will." The man tapped the document in front of him.

"Why would an investor include me in his will?"

"Buck was more than just an investor, Darius. He was…your father."

The room became eerily quiet. The only sound was the ticking of the grandfather clock on the wall behind him.

Darius stared at the man a few moments longer, sure someone would pop through the door and declare that this was a prank.

"Look, Mr. LeBlanc—"

"Kace."

"Kace…there must be some mix-up. You've got the wrong guy."

"You're Darius Taylor-Pratt, son of former actress

Liberty Taylor. Adopted by your stepfather, William Pratt, at the age of two. You're thirty years old, and you received your undergrad at—"

"All right." Darius held up a hand. He wanted Kace to stop talking long enough for him to wrap his head around what was happening. He sucked in a deep breath and tried to slow his rocketing heart rate. "You're saying that this guy, this…"

"Buckley Blackwood."

"…and my mother…they were *together* at some point."

"Yes."

"He knew I was his son. Yet, he never so much as called or dropped a birthday card in the mail in thirty years." Anger slowly crept up his spine. "Why? Was he ashamed that he'd fathered a son by a black woman?"

"No," Kace responded emphatically. "That wasn't it at all."

"Then what was it *exactly*?" Darius seethed, unconvinced.

"You were the product of an affair during his first marriage. That's why he thought it best to care for you from a distance. When you were two, and your mother married Mr. Pratt, Buck agreed to allow him to adopt you and raise you as his son. You were to be informed of the adoption once you turned eighteen, which I assume you were."

Darius gripped the armrest without response, his head pounding and his muscles tense.

He'd been told that Will wasn't his biological father. But his mother wouldn't reveal his father's identity beyond saying he was a wealthy man who didn't want to "complicate" his life.

"Darius," the man said, "I realize this must come as a shock to you, but—"

"That's the understatement of the year, Mr. LeBlanc." He gritted the words through clenched teeth.

"Just Kace is fine," the man insisted.

Darius was beginning to hate Kace's sympathetic expression. It felt a lot like condescension and pity.

"The old man is dead, so I'm obviously not here for a father-son reunion." The declaration made him sound like a heartless ass, but Buckley Blackwood had shown him the same callous disregard. "And you could've conducted the reading of the will via video conference. So why the hell am I really here?"

"I'll allow Buck to explain for himself." Kace read the final will and testament of Buckley Blackwood. The more he read, the more agitated Darius became.

Buckley Blackwood was a coward and an asshole.

Too cowardly to claim him as his son while he was alive. And the kind of jerk who left everything to his pretty, young ex-wife while leaving nothing to his children. And just for shits and giggles, Darius was being asked to take a DNA test to prove he was Buck's son.

"Any questions?" Kace put down the will and clasped his hands on the desk. The man seemed braced for a verbal assault.

"What's the point of a DNA test? The man's dead, and it's not as if I'm in line to inherit anything."

"You have three siblings." Kace laid out the photos individually. "Kellan, Vaughn and Sophie."

Darius's mouth went dry, and he couldn't speak. He wanted to shove the photos onto the floor and call bullshit on this entire charade.

But he couldn't.

Darius picked up each photo and studied it.

His brown skin was darker than theirs, but they shared many facial features.

His nose, chin and cheekbones were similar to theirs, and he and Sophie had the same rich brown eyes.

An unexpected sense of belonging washed over him, like a wave at high tide, with the power to knock him off his feet. He swallowed hard, returning each photo to the mahogany desk.

"Do they know about me?"

"They learned of you after their father's death."

"Does anyone else know?"

"So far, just the family," Kace said.

"Good. Let's keep it that way." A knot tightened in his gut. The same one he'd developed when he'd gone to school with wealthy kids who'd treated him like an undeserving outsider.

He'd learned to relish that status. Had incorporated it into the Thr3d brand. But he wasn't keen on experiencing that kind of painful rejection again. Especially not from people with whom he shared DNA.

Darius wanted to walk out. Refuse to play along with the old man's sick game. But a part of him *needed* answers. And this was the only way he'd finally get them.

"I'll take the test."

"They're expecting you at Royal Memorial Hospital." Kace slid a sheet of paper across the desk, then closed the folder. "As for the estate…from what I've learned about you, you've always been a fighter. Two of your siblings are contesting the will. I'm certainly not encouraging you to do so, but—"

"It is an option." Darius rubbed his jaw.

Kace gave him a subtle nod. "I'll be in touch when

I get the DNA results. In the meantime, someone else would like to speak with you. Should I send her in?"

Darius nodded absently, not really listening. He pulled his phone from his pocket once the door clicked shut behind Kace. He needed to tell his mother and stepfather he finally knew the truth about his paternity. But they were on vacation. And this wasn't the kind of conversation they should have over the phone while they were an ocean away. He'd wait until they returned from Europe and talk to them in person.

His relationship with them had been strained since he'd learned that Will wasn't his biological father. He could've forgiven that lie. Maybe even understood it. But when his mother refused to reveal the identity of his father, Darius had been furious.

Now he knew the truth.

He was the son of some rich asshole who hadn't wanted him when he was alive but felt the need to alleviate his conscience on his deathbed.

The door opened suddenly, startling him.

"Hello, Darius. It's a pleasure to finally meet you." Miranda Dupree extended a hand.

He scrambled to his feet and shook her hand. She was nearly a foot shorter than him. "Pleasure to meet you, Ms. Dupree."

"Call me Miranda, and please, have a seat." She settled onto the chair beside him. "I apologize for not being direct about why I invited you here." She sifted her fingers through her wavy red hair. Her sparkling, deep blue eyes seemed sincere. "But I didn't think you'd come if I'd told you the truth."

True.

But that didn't earn her a pass for lying to him.

"So the collaboration was just a ruse?"

"I prefer to think of it as bait." Miranda smiled sweetly. "What I said about wanting to create a signature clothing line…that's absolutely true. I'd like to revisit the topic once all of this is sorted out."

He acknowledged her statement with a slight nod. But his head still swirled with the news of his paternity.

So much for those fantasies of a reunion with my long-lost father.

"Darius…" Miranda placed a gentle hand on his forearm. "I can only imagine what you must be feeling."

"Then I'll tell you." He glared at her. "I feel like I'm being manipulated. By you. By that lawyer. And by a gutless old man who never gave a damn about me when he was alive but wants to play God with my life now that he's dead."

Miranda seemed willing to absorb his anger, her gaze still warm and sincere. "If I was in your shoes, I'd probably feel the same. But there's something you need to see."

Miranda retrieved a thick envelope from the desk and sat beside him again.

"Buck and I hadn't spoken much since our divorce. So I was as shocked as anyone that he charged me with handling some very sensitive matters after his death. I've received more instructions via letters over the past few months. Yes, the man could be an asshole." She laughed bitterly. "But one of his deepest regrets was never getting to know you. He implored me to bring you here, so you'd have the opportunity to get to know your brothers and sister. And he wanted you to know that, regardless of what you might believe, you were never far from his thoughts."

"He had a damn funny way of showing it."

"Buck struggled to show affection with everyone. It destroyed both of his marriages. And it's the reason his relationships with his children were strained. The reason he died alone." She frowned. "But it doesn't mean he didn't care about you."

Miranda handed him the envelope. "Buck wanted you to have this…to know that even though you were apart, he always held you in his heart."

She stood. "I'll leave you alone with it. You can review it here for now. Once the DNA results have been confirmed, it's yours to keep. When you're ready, my driver will take you anywhere you'd like to go. I've reserved a furnished rental home in town for you. It's yours for as long as you need it."

Miranda handed him two business cards. "If you need me or Kace, just give us a call. I'll be in touch."

Once Miranda was gone, he opened the envelope. It held a scrapbook overflowing with photos and newspaper articles. On the first page, there was a photo of a newborn he recognized as himself. A duplicate was in his mother's prized photo album.

Darius made his way through the scrapbook one aged photo, yellowed newspaper clipping and dog-eared magazine article at a time.

The man had been following his childhood, his academic career and his business triumphs. Yet, he hadn't reached out to him once in thirty years.

What am I supposed to feel for a man like that?

Darius dropped the scrapbook onto the desk, slipped his Prada shades back on and met Miranda's driver, Leslie, at the car.

"Where shall I take you, sir?" She opened the door. "Back to the airport or to your rental home?"

Darius slid into the back seat. "Neither. Take me someplace I can get a decent hamburger, fries and shake, please."

He wasn't sure what he'd do next. He only knew that he thought better on a full stomach, and he longed for the comfort of carbs while he plotted his next move.

Two

Darius stepped inside the quaint little Royal Diner. The place looked like a throwback from the fifties, with its red faux-leather booths and black-and-white checkerboard linoleum tile floor.

He ordered a mile-high bacon cheeseburger, wedge fries and a thick, handmade strawberry shake. The same meal he'd ordered when his mother and Will would take him out to eat after a big win or a devastating loss.

It was still his go-to meal for either.

And today he found himself thinking of his mother and stepfather more than he had in months.

He was furious that his mother hadn't told him Buckley Blackwood was his biological father. But part of him missed the great hugs his mom gave whenever he'd had a bad day. And the corny jokes Will would tell to lift his spirits.

But then, they hadn't distanced themselves from him. He'd pulled away from them because they'd been lying to him his entire life.

Buckley Blackwood was just another lying parent who only revealed the truth when it was convenient. Darius already had a bookend set of those.

He should feel badly that he'd never meet his biological father. But the only thing he felt toward Blackwood was resentment. The man could've picked up the telephone or flown his private plane to reach him at any point in the past thirty years.

He'd *chosen* not to. Not even when he was dying and knew he had only weeks to live. Instead, he'd apparently spent the end of his life concocting this manipulative scheme.

But to what end?

Amanda Battle, the woman who'd introduced herself as the owner of the little diner, brought him his meal and shake. He nibbled on one of the fries, dipping it into the ketchup he'd poured on his plate.

Darius had spent the past twelve years musing about his mysterious biological father. Right now, he wanted to hate the man. But the scrapbook Miranda had given him didn't correspond with the heartless man he'd imagined.

It wasn't just that the old man had been collecting photos, news clippings and such about Darius his entire life. The photos showed signs of frequent handling. The dog-eared magazine articles appeared to have been read repeatedly. It was the kind of scrapbook he'd expect from a parent who actually gave a damn about his kid.

He sighed, nibbling on more fries. The two sides of the man who was likely his father were incongruent, at best. But clipping out a few magazine articles didn't excuse Blackwood for being a shitty, absent father.

For that, he would never forgive him.

Darius took another of the wedge fries, swiped it in the milkshake and popped it in his mouth.

It was something people over the age of twelve usually found repulsive. But today, he deserved to indulge himself.

"A bacon cheeseburger, fries and a strawberry shake. I was going to ask if it was a really good day or a really bad one, but then you dipped your fry into your shake, so I guess that answers that."

Darius froze, then turned toward the familiar voice. His eyes widened.

"Audra Lee Covington?"

No, it isn't possible.

What would his grad school girlfriend be doing in Royal, Texas?

"So you do remember me." She folded her arms. "I wasn't sure you would. After all, you never returned my calls."

Remember? He couldn't forget her if he tried. She'd been his biggest regret. The woman who still haunted his dreams.

He stared at her, blinking. Still not sure he could believe his eyes.

She was stunning, as always. Her dark wavy hair was tucked behind her ears and fell to her shoulders. Gold-and-diamond starburst ear climbers decorated the outer curve of each ear. She wore a cream-colored, chunky-knit sweater and distressed skinny jeans that hugged every curve. And there was a small, star-shaped diamond stud in one nostril.

"Audra." He stood, wiping his hands on a napkin. He inhaled her sweet scent as they shared an awkward hug. "What on earth are you doing here?"

"Good to see you, too," she said sarcastically as she stepped away, folding her arms again. Her lips pressed into a harsh line as she narrowed her gaze at him.

If looks could kill, he'd be laid out on the black-and-white tile floor with a chalk line around him.

"It's good to see you, Audra, of course. I should've said I'm stunned to see you here in Royal, Texas." He gestured toward the opposite side of the booth. "You look…amazing." It was an egregious understatement. She was drop-dead gorgeous. "Join me?"

Audra's sensual lips, shiny with lip gloss, quirked in a semi-frown as she studied him. Finally, she nodded and slid across from him in the booth.

"The new look—" she indicated his bald head, a look he'd transitioned to nearly three years ago "—I like it. It suits you."

"Thanks." He cleared his throat. "What did you order?"

"They make an incredible Cobb salad. It probably has as many calories as your burger and fries, but at least I feel like I'm making an effort."

He'd always loved her refreshing honesty. Too bad he hadn't afforded her the same. Their story still would've ended. But if he'd been honest with her then, at least he'd have no regrets where Audra was concerned.

"LA Fashion Week is just a few weeks away. I'd expect the great Audra Lee Covington to be in the design studio right now."

Audra was a diamond heiress. She'd broken rank with her very traditional family and formed her own company that catered to a younger, trendier clientele. Her name got frequent mentions in fashion magazines when A-list actors, musicians and social influencers bragged that they were iced in Audra Lee Covington diamond earrings, necklaces, bracelets and tiaras.

"Royal isn't my usual hangout. That's for sure." A deep smile lit Audra's rich espresso-brown eyes, the same color as her shoulder-length hair. "I got an early start on the season this year. So when I received a lucrative request from a wealthy bride-to-be here in Royal, I couldn't resist. I'm creating custom wedding jewelry for the couple and gifts for their bridal party. So I'm staying in town for a bit. Getting to know the area and the bride, who will be returning from New York tomorrow with her fiancé. I'd hardly expect to run into you here, either." She clasped her hands on the table. "I hear Thr3d will be doing a runway show this year."

"We are. My team is back in LA working tirelessly to prepare for it."

She produced a gum-filled lollipop from her pocket, opened the wrapper and popped it in her mouth.

Was that a fucking tongue ring?

Darius was pretty sure his jaw hit the ground and another part of his body reached for the sky.

Good thing he'd returned to his seat.

Audra propped her elbows on the table and tilted her head as she studied him. "What brings you to Royal?"

"A business opportunity." It wasn't a lie. The opportunity to collaborate with Miranda had brought him to town.

She sucked on that damn lollipop, which had already stained her tongue red, and awaited further explanation.

"It's too early to share details." He picked up his

burger. "But I'm hoping to create a clothing line for a major fitness brand."

"Ah." When she said it, he couldn't help staring at her candy-red, pierced tongue. "Miranda Dupree. Scoring the clothing line for her Goddess brand would be a major coup."

"How'd you—"

"It's a small world, I guess." She shrugged. "Miranda is my client's ex-stepmother. My client is Sophie Blackwood. Do you know her?"

His half sister. Damn. It *was* a small world.

"Never met her." He shrugged. "But I've heard the name."

Less than an hour ago, in fact.

Audra's mouth made a popping sound when she yanked the lollipop from between her lips. She stared at him, her brown eyes narrowed. Judging him. As if she didn't believe him.

Darius bit a mouthful of the bacon cheeseburger.

He hadn't seen Audra in five years. They weren't together, and she had no right to know his personal business.

So why did he feel as guilty now for telling her a half-truth as he had when they were together?

Audra returned the sucker to her mouth and rose from the table. She didn't believe him, but she obviously didn't deem pursuing the truth worth her time.

Knowing she found him unworthy made his chest ache. Her wordless condemnation was exactly what he deserved.

"Looks like they're done with my order." Audra nodded toward where Amanda was packing a to-go bag.

"Nice seeing you again, Darius. Good luck with Fashion Week."

Darius groaned quietly as he swiped another French fry into his milkshake and took a bite.

Audra made a hasty escape, and he couldn't blame her.

He was a liar. Apparently, it was hereditary.

Three

Audra slid into the driver's seat of the Bentley Continental GT convertible her parents had gifted her four years ago, after her business cleared a million dollars in profits in its first year.

She glanced back at the diner. Darius sat motionless in the booth where she'd left him.

Of all the people in the world that she could run into, she had to run into Darius Freaking Taylor-Pratt. The man who'd broken her heart five years ago.

She'd been madly in love with him, and she'd believed he loved her, too. Right up to the moment he'd said things had gotten too serious between them, and he needed space.

There had been no discussion. No evidence he'd fallen for someone else. And no real explanation.

She'd been devastated.

They'd met at a party during grad school at Harvard. The attraction between them had almost been instant. She'd told her friend that she was pretty sure she'd met the man she was going to marry.

Sure, she'd been a little buzzed when she said it. But every day they were together made her believe those words to be true.

Darius suddenly ending things had come of out nowhere. It had left her reeling, wondering what she'd done wrong.

But that was the past. It'd taken some time, but she'd gotten over it and moved on.

Or at least she'd always believed she had. But seeing Darius today made her feel as if things between them weren't finished at all.

He was more handsome than ever in his navy Tom Ford suit, a white shirt and a navy print tie. His story about being in Royal on business was undoubtedly true. Never a fan of suits, Darius would require a damn good reason to wear one.

And the bald head he was rocking...on him it was sexy as sin. Her fingers had itched with the desire to run her palm over the smooth, brown skin on his clean-shaven head. She'd balled her hands into fists, her fingernails leaving marks on her palms.

Darius's dark brown eyes registered a mix of emotions she couldn't quite read.

Sadness. Anger? Maybe even regret.

The only thing she knew for sure was that she'd desperately wanted to lean in and kiss him. If only to remind him of what he'd walked away from five years ago.

Her cell phone rang.

Sophie Blackwood.

Audra smiled, thankful for the distraction. She hit the call button and pulled out of her parking space, heading back toward the house she was renting while she stayed in Royal.

"Hello, Sophie. Back in town yet?"

"We arrived a couple of hours ago. Nigel, my fiancé, needed to stay a couple more days to take care of a staffing issue with the show."

Audra couldn't help smiling. Sophie was doing that thing that many newly engaged women did where they referred to their intended as their *fiancé*, as frequently as possible. It was adorable. And everything about Sophie's bubbly excitement and the warmth with which she talked about him spoke to just how in love they were.

For Sophie's sake, Audra truly hoped that their love would last.

"No worries. I've been keeping myself occupied. I sketched out a few designs. I'll show them to you when we get together."

"Are you busy now? We're going to grab a bite with friends over at the Glass House in an hour or so. You should join us."

"Thanks, but I just picked up a salad." Hopefully, Sophie didn't think her rude for turning down her offer.

"Is everything all right?" Sophie's voice was laced with concern.

"Yes. I'm just a bit stunned. I ran into my grad school ex just now."

"A local?" Sophie asked.

"No, in fact, I got the impression this is his first time here, too. So it was weird to run into him." Audra bit into the sucker she'd teased Darius with.

She was pretty sure he'd nearly fainted when he caught a glimpse of her pierced tongue.

Good.

She might be over Darius, but she wasn't above reminding him that he should be sorry he'd walked out on her.

"Oh? Who is he?" Sophie's voice sounded less jovial.

"Darius Taylor-Pratt. He runs the athletic performance clothing company Thr3d."

"That must've been quite a surprise." Sophie laughed nervously, then quickly changed the subject. "So the venue where I'd like to have my wedding got damaged during the recent wildfires. The damaged portions have been rebuilt, but there's still a lot of work to do. If you could spare the time this Saturday, we could definitely use the help. Besides, it would be a chance for you to get to know some of the folks you're creating custom jewelry pieces for."

"Sure." Audra shrugged. "And maybe we can meet tomorrow afternoon to discuss your custom designs?"

"Come to my place tomorrow afternoon at one. We'll have a late lunch and go over everything." Full-blown giddiness had returned to Sophie's voice. "See you then!"

God, I remember what it felt like to be that in love.

Seeing Darius and talking to Sophie made her even more certain she'd done the right thing when she'd broken it off with her most recent ex a few months ago.

Cassius "Cash" Johannsson was *exactly* the man her mother and United States senator father wanted her to marry. A perfectly nice gentleman from the right family with ambitions to one day sit in the Oval Office. But she wanted more than just "perfectly nice."

She wanted a man who made her laugh. Who was her friend as well as her lover. A man who understood the manic craziness that often accompanied a creative mind. A man who made her body burn for his.

Cash had never engendered that kind of spark in her. Nor had she ever gushed over Cash the way Sophie did over Nigel. The way she once had over Darius.

In the end, she'd broken it off with Cash because she was just settling. He deserved someone who would feel like the luckiest girl in the world to be on his arm.

Audra entered the beautiful gated community where her rental house was located. She was traveling with sample jewelry pieces and loose diamonds, the value of which easily topped two million dollars. So she required the additional security afforded by this gated community and the safety measures of the home she was renting from the Blackwoods' family friend—Dixie Musgraves.

She grabbed her meal, courtesy of the Royal Diner, and headed inside, determined to banish all thoughts of Darius.

Four

It already felt like the longest day of Darius's life, and he still had a few hours of work ahead of him. He settled behind the glass-and-steel desk in the office of his rental home and prepared for yet another conference call. This one with his production manager and a few key members of the production staff.

The preparations for LA Fashion Week had to go off without a hitch. This would be Thr3d's first runway show at the event. And he was determined it wouldn't be the last.

It was an honor to get a runway show for his athletic gear. One he wouldn't squander. And if everything went as expected, buyers in untapped markets would order the Thr3d fall line for their stores. So despite the issues with his paternity and his biological father's estate, he wouldn't allow himself to be distracted.

Fifteen minutes into the conversation with his team, he heard water splash.

Darius walked over to the bank of windows along the back wall of the office and stared down. There was a woman swimming in his pool.

"Boss? Boss?" His production manager Leeson Brown was saying.

"Oh… I…uh…" He cleared his throat. "Sorry. Didn't catch that last part."

"I said unless you have something else for us, that pretty much covers everything," Lee repeated. "Don't worry. The entire team understands the importance of this show. We won't let you down."

"I know you won't." Darius watched the woman's movements. There was something oddly familiar about her strong, elegant strokes.

Who is she and what the hell is she doing here?

"The team is doing a great job," Darius assured Lee. "I'll touch base soon. But if you run into any problems…"

"We won't hesitate to call," Lee assured him.

"Day or night," Darius told the man as his gaze followed the woman swimming laps in his pool.

"I promise. In the meantime, I know it's a tall order for you, but try to relax."

Darius promised he would try. Then he slipped the phone into his pocket and headed down to the pool to find out who was trespassing on the Blackwoods' property and distracting him from his work.

As he made his way across the patio, the woman climbed out of the pool in a tiny bikini that showed off her delicious curves. She tugged the cap off her head and tossed it on a lounge chair and bent over to grab her beach towel.

Good. God. Almighty.

This woman's behind was a museum-worthy work of art.

"Excuse me," he said, finally.

Startled, the woman dropped her towel and whipped around, her eyes widening.

"Darius?"

"Audra?"

They spoke simultaneously. Then Darius added, "Did you follow me back here?"

She propped a fist on one generous hip, drawing his attention to her belly button piercing and the connected gold chain looped around her waist. "Do you honestly believe I need to resort to following random dudes home?"

Ouch.

She'd just called him a *random dude*. As if he didn't matter to her and never really had.

Audra didn't wait for his response. She snatched the towel off the lounge chair and dried herself. Doubtless, the pool was heated, but the temperature outside had cooled considerably. She was shivering.

He couldn't help thinking of the last time he'd seen her shivering. She'd been lying beneath him, gloriously naked. He swallowed hard. Heat crawled up his neck and face.

"Does that mean you're renting this house now?" She pulled a short, black cover-up over her head and slipped her arms inside before plopping down on the end of the lounger to dry her hair. "Because it was empty when I went for a swim this morning."

"My business will keep me here a few more days." He shoved a hand in his pocket. "Miranda offered me this place for as long as I need it."

Darius surveyed the well-manicured patio with its lovely landscaping and the pool complete with a hot tub and water feature. He'd paid little attention to the backyard during the cursory tour Leslie had given him when she'd deposited him here a couple of hours ago.

He'd been in the office, sifting through emails or on one call after another, ever since. Starting with the call he'd placed to his attorney, apprising him of the situation and charging the man with exploring his options.

Darius didn't need Buckley Blackwood's money. His athletic clothing line was one of the fastest-growing companies of its kind in the US, and it was already making millions each year. If Thr3d maintained its current trajectory, it was positioned to climb its way to being one of the top ten athletic wear companies in the country within ten years.

Still, Darius felt compelled to fight for some portion of the estate—to demand acknowledgment as a Blackwood heir. Even if he simply donated the money to a worthy cause. But he wasn't prepared to tell Audra any of that. There was no reason for him to tell his pedigreed ex that he was a bastard child. The product of an illicit affair between an asshole banker and a failed actress. An inconvenience neither of them had planned for or wanted.

"How long will you be in Royal?" Audra stood, her towel folded over her arm. She didn't sound happy about him staying in town.

"It's hard to say right now." He shoved his hands in

his pockets and leaned against the edge of the hot tub. "You?"

"Same." Audra slipped her feet into her bejeweled flip-flops. "But my client Sophie and her fiancé are back in town. I should be able to make some serious progress in the next week or two."

He sucked in a deep breath at the mention of his half sister's name. After lying to Audra about his family in the past, he hated the idea of keeping this secret from her, even if they weren't together. But he wasn't prepared to air his family's dirty laundry. Especially when his paternity had yet to be definitively proven.

"Great," he said. "But that doesn't explain why you're in my pool. You aren't staying here, too, are you?"

"Heaven forbid." Audra pressed an open hand to her chest in feigned outrage. She nodded toward the house on the other side of the brick wall. "I'm renting the darling house next door. It has a proper workshop, great office space and plenty of security. But it doesn't have a pool, and back home in Dallas I swim nearly every day."

"You're in Dallas now?"

"I moved there after grad school." She shrugged. "I needed a fresh start and Dallas felt right."

Guilt churned in his gut. *Did she need a fresh start because of our breakup?*

"Anyway, Sophie gave me permission to use this pool since her family owns the house and it's empty. At least it *was* empty. In light of everything that's been going on with her father's death and the estate going to her stepmother... I'm sure Sophie had no idea you were staying here."

"Makes sense." He stared at her, unable to tear his gaze from her expressive eyes. He wanted to take her in his arms and get reacquainted with every one of her sensual curves.

"Sorry I disturbed you." She broke their gaze. "I'm sure there's another pool in town I could use."

"No. You don't need to do that." He objected far too quickly, and he couldn't help but notice she was restraining a smile. "You aren't bothering me. I only came out because I thought you were a trespasser." He folded his arms. "Come over whenever you want. I doubt I'll be using the pool while I'm here."

"That's a shame." She shrugged. "My time in the pool relaxes me and sparks my creativity. You should try it."

"You're shivering. Can I make you some coffee or tea? Hot cocoa, maybe?" He gestured toward the house.

What the hell was he thinking?

The last thing he needed was to spend *more* time with Audra. Yet, he wanted her to stay a little while longer. Even if it meant he'd lie awake all night, revisiting his regrets.

But he could never go back. There were no do-overs in romantic or family relationships. He'd burned that bridge when he'd walked away from her.

"That's kind of you." She managed a polite smile. "But I'll be plenty warm between the hot bubble bath with my name on it and the Sex on the Beach I plan to have…the drink, not the actual—"

"Of course." He ran a hand over his clean-shaven head.

But all he could think about was that time they'd gone to Martha's Vineyard and ended up having sex on the beach.

It wasn't nearly as glamorous as people made it out

to be. They'd both gotten sand in places sand should never, *ever* be. But they'd had fun that night. A night he'd never forget.

Audra began ordering Sex on the Beach cocktails after that. Initially, as a private joke between them which ignited that passionate memory. But then she'd actually started to like them, and it became her signature drink.

As they stood awkwardly staring at one another, he wondered if she still regarded the memory fondly. Or was every memory of what they once shared now tainted?

"Thank you for letting me use the pool. I'll try not to disturb you. Good night."

"Good night," he called to her retreating back.

Audra disappeared through the iron gate that connected the two backyards.

Darius rubbed a hand over his head and groaned. The universe had it in for him. He was sure of it.

The collaboration project with Goddess had turned out to be a ruse to get him to Royal. He'd finally— *probably*—discovered who his father was, but the selfish bastard had gone and died before Darius had a chance to tell him to go to hell. The man was richer than God but hadn't left any of his children a dime. Darius had siblings, but with them already fighting Miranda on the will, he doubted they would appreciate a surprise heir popping up out of the woodwork.

And then there's Audra.

Not only was she right here in Royal, but she was staying next door and using his pool wearing a scrap of fabric masquerading as a bikini.

Yep. Either he was being punked or the universe was having a nice laugh at his expense.

His eyes were drawn to the light that suddenly went on upstairs in the house next door.

Audra.

Probably drawing a bubble bath with her Sex on the Beach in hand.

He shut his eyes against the erotic images that flooded his brain, his body stiffening in response.

There would be a lot of cold showers and sleepless nights in his future.

Audra dropped her damp towel in the laundry bin and went to the kitchen to retrieve the pitcher of cocktails she'd made earlier and put in the fridge.

She'd mixed her favorite drink the moment she'd returned home after seeing Darius. It was bad enough he was in the same Texas town where she was. Did he have to be staying next door, too?

Audra pulled out a glass and filled it, the liquid sloshing onto the counter.

Her hands were shaking.

She sucked in a deep breath, her eyes drifting closed.

"Of all the goddamn places in the world he could possibly be," she muttered under her breath as she wiped up the mess.

Not that it mattered.

She was over Darius. So it didn't matter how good he looked in those black basketball pants and a heather-gray performance shirt emblazoned with the Thr3d logo. A shirt that clung to the muscles of his chest and biceps.

He was her past. A mistake she'd never repeat.

But God, parts of her wanted to. And right now, those parts were drowning out her common sense, which reminded her that she should know better.

She went upstairs and turned on the warm water, adding some of the decadent bath foam with a heavenly crème brûlée scent. It was pricey, but it left her skin incredibly soft and smelling sweet. And the luxurious bubbles it created were perfect for a day like this.

Audra stripped out of her wet bikini and removed the belly chain before slipping beneath the scented bubbles.

Her phone rang. Because…of course it would. She sat up and peeked at the caller ID.

Cash.

She groaned as she slipped beneath the water again.

Some much-needed distance from her ex, who still didn't seem to understand it was over, was the real reason she'd found Sophie Blackwood's project so intriguing. Audra looked forward to immersing herself completely in the project without the possibility of running into her ex or seeing the local politician's face splashed across television commercials and on the side of buses.

The chorus of the old George Strait song, "All My Ex's Live in Texas," a favorite of her grandfather's, suddenly came to her and she couldn't help laughing.

Cash was a good guy. She honestly felt badly about ignoring his call. But she simply didn't have the energy to deal with another ex tonight.

Besides, how many more ways can I explain that it's over?

Audra wouldn't change her mind. She didn't care that their mothers had been hoping for a match between them since she and Cash were teens, and their fathers had served together as senators.

Their relationship seemed picture-perfect from the outside—like the chocolate shell on the outside of a cherry cordial. But on the inside, there were no cherries and there was no cream filling. There was nothing at all beyond the surface, leaving her with a hollow, empty feeling.

She needed something more.

Something like what she and Darius had shared. But this time, with someone who *wanted* to be with her. Always.

The way she'd once felt about Darius.

Her phone signaled that she had a new voice mail and she sighed quietly. For the first time, she understood why Darius hadn't returned her calls five years ago.

When it's really over, what else is there to discuss?

The realization made her heart ache. No matter how much she tried to deny it, a part of her heart still harbored the small hope that she and Darius could one day get it right.

That was why she'd turned down his invitation to join him for coffee. She needed to protect the fragile part of her heart that held on to that hope.

She gave her phone the voice command to play the eighties and nineties soft rock music playlist that always relaxed her.

Steve Perry sang the opening lines of "Foolish Heart."

It was just the reminder she needed.

You're here for one reason and one reason only. Stay focused.

Anything else was a foolish distraction that would only lead to a broken heart.

She'd had enough of those to last a lifetime.

Five

It was his second day in Royal. Despite barely sleeping four hours last night, he'd risen early this morning to the sound of Audra diving into the pool. He'd gotten up, taken a quick shower, dressed, grabbed a cup of coffee and then watched her graceful movements as she finished her laps.

When she was done, she toweled off and made her way back to her yard without casting so much as a glance toward the house.

Not that he wanted or expected her to look for him. But he certainly hadn't been able to take his eyes off of her.

The swimsuit she'd worn that morning was a one-piece, long-sleeve suit with a zipper down the front. Suitable for the chillier early-morning temperature. But he couldn't help thinking of how amazing she'd looked in the two-piece she'd worn last night.

He was groggy and jetlagged. Restless, because it was still too early to call any of his team back home in LA. But watching Audra for the past two days had given him an idea. Swimwear for both men and women.

When he'd originally started the line five years ago, it had consisted of a handful of men's sportswear pieces. Little by little, he'd expanded the collection. Two years ago, they'd tested their first women's collection. It had been a resounding success. But neither line included swimwear.

It was risky to throw something else into the mix so close to their first LA Fashion Week runway show. But if they could pull it off, the swimwear pieces might even become the centerpiece of the show.

Darius pulled out his sketchpad and the wooden case that contained his watercolor pencils. He drafted a rough outline of a woman's suit adorning the shapely curves that had inspired the idea. The same ones that haunted his sleep.

Audra couldn't help smiling as she sat across the table from Sophie Blackwood and her fiancé, Nigel Townshend. They made a handsome couple.

Sophie had long, glossy auburn hair, warm brown eyes and killer curves, highlighted by the peplum blouse she wore coupled with a maxi skirt.

Nigel's stunning, baby blue eyes practically danced as he watched Sophie. He sat with an arm wrapped around his fiancée's waist. His mouth curved in a contented smile.

The two of them were beyond adorable.

And as if the man wasn't handsome enough with his good looks and his short, tousled brown hair, he spoke with a thick British accent. Audra could happily listen to Nigel Townshend recite the periodic table.

After lunch, they'd moved to a sun-filled room just off the patio. Where Sophie and Nigel shared their vision for their wedding rings and the custom jewelry pieces they wanted to give each member of their bridal party. Audra took notes and sketched in her notebook as the couple talked. She loved hearing the funny, sweet and moving stories about the friends and family they'd selected to stand beside them on their wedding day.

This was why she loved working with engaged couples. It reminded her true love really existed.

She'd thought she'd found the love of her life the night she met Darius. But she'd been wrong. Then she'd taken the expected path by getting into a relationship with Cash. But getting involved with her longtime family friend had been a mistake, too.

Working with couples like Sophie and Nigel revived her belief that, regardless of her failures and false starts, she'd eventually find the man she'd want to be with forever.

Someone who'd feel the same about her.

As they chatted, Audra made a few amendments to the three concepts she'd developed for Sophie's and Nigel's rings.

"Okay," Audra said finally, her heart beating a mile a minute. "Here are a few options for your engagement and wedding rings. They're just preliminary sketches that'll give me a better sense of the right design for you." She turned the sketchpad toward the couple and pushed it across the table tentatively. "What do you think? Am I on the right track?"

Audra was good at what she did, and she'd designed hundreds of pieces over the past five years. But it always made her incredibly nervous to show clients her first draft. This moment could make or break the rest of the design experience.

"Oh my God." Sophie pressed a trembling hand to her lips. Her eyes filled with tears as she traced the sketch of the vintage-inspired, floral-themed engagement ring. "It's stunning. I love it." She gripped Nigel's forearm and gazed up at him. "What do you think?"

"I couldn't possibly imagine a better reaction." He beamed, wiping tears from her cheek with his thumb. "So I'm happy if you're happy, love."

It was sweet of Nigel, but it wasn't the enthusiastic reaction Audra was hoping for. He obviously didn't care for the corresponding design for his ring. Instead, his eye was drawn to the sketch of a set of sleek, modern wedding bands.

They were a stark contrast to the engagement ring Sophie adored.

"I realize that tradition dictates matching wedding bands, but this is *your* life and *your* marriage," Audra said. "Who says you have to be bound by tradition?"

"You're suggesting we have different styles of wedding bands?" Sophie asked.

"Why not?" Audra shrugged. "Your differences are part of what attracted you two, right? Why not celebrate them by selecting individual ring styles connected by the same metals?"

"Bloody brilliant, Audra." Nigel grinned. He turned back to Sophie. "What do you think, love?"

"I love the symbolism of it." Sophie sounded unconvinced as she pressed a hand to her cheek.

Translation: she hates the idea.

"It would be better if I showed you." Audra smiled confidently. "I'll have new sketches ready for you tomorrow afternoon. And I'll bring samples so you can get a better sense of how the finished design will look."

"Thank you." The joy returned to Sophie's eyes.

Audra gathered her sketchbook and pencils. "I'd better get back to my office and get started."

Nigel excused himself to take a call, and Sophie walked her toward the door.

"So that was crazy, you running into your ex here, huh?" Sophie said.

Audra halted at the mention of Darius, but feigned indifference. "It was, but what was even more bizarre is that when I went for a swim last night, I discovered he's staying at the house next door while he's in town."

"Wait…why is he staying there?"

"He's in Royal on business with your former stepmother. She owns the property now, right? I guess she's putting him up there while he's in town."

"I see." Sophie frowned. "I wonder what kind of business they have together."

Audra didn't answer. It wasn't her place to reveal what Darius had shared with her about his potential deal with Miranda.

"What was it like seeing him again after all these years?" Sophie asked.

"Weird, I guess, is the best way to describe it." Audra shrugged, though emotion welled in her chest. "He broke my heart, but we didn't part on bad terms. He simply made the choice to walk away."

"Did he leave you for someone else?"

"That's just it, I don't believe he did." Audra lifted the strap of her bag higher on her shoulder. "He just didn't want to be with me anymore. Honestly? It hurt like hell, but I get it. It's the same reason I broke it off with my recent ex. He's a perfectly good guy. He just isn't the one I want to spend a lifetime with."

"But Darius was. Wasn't he?" Sophie placed a comforting hand on Audra's arm.

Something about the younger woman's offer of comfort moved Audra. Tears welled in her eyes. She blinked them away. "I thought so at the time, but later I learned that he hadn't been honest with me about something important."

"Like?" Sophie asked tentatively.

They weren't friends. Sophie was her client. But Audra had a compelling need to talk to *someone* about this.

"He told me his parents were dead. A few years later, I read a magazine article where he said he had an estranged relationship with his mother and stepfather. But they were very much alive." Audra dragged her fingers through her hair and sighed. "What kind of man would lie about something like that?"

"That is curious." Sophie frowned. "But perhaps he had a good reason. Did you confront him about it?"

"It was over between us, and I hadn't seen him in years by then." Audra shrugged. "What would be the point?"

"He obviously meant a lot to you," Sophie said in a hushed tone as Nigel approached. "Now that you've reconnected—"

"We *haven't* reconnected," Audra corrected her.

"Okay. Now that you two are neighbors and on friendly terms…" Sophie shrugged. "If it was me, I'd want to know."

Of course I want to know why Darius lied to me about his parents.

But demanding an explanation from him now would only make him believe she still cared. Which she didn't. Because she was definitely over him.

"I'd better be going. Thank you both for a lovely lunch." Audra smiled politely but didn't acknowledge Sophie's comment.

Audra focused on the short drive back to her rental house in the same community of Pine Valley. A small part of her was envious of Sophie and Nigel. She didn't begrudge them their happiness. She just wanted a little of that bliss for herself.

Six

Darius had been so busy working on the swimwear designs that he'd lost track of time. He didn't realize how late it was until the setting of the sun forced him to turn on the lights.

He left his makeshift drafting table and sat at his computer to catch up on an email chain circulating between members of his team.

They'd been stunned during a video conference that morning when he'd announced the addition of swimwear to the runway show collection. First there was silence, except for his production chief Leeson. The man laughed, thinking Darius must be joking.

When he realized Darius was serious, Lee's chuckles gave way to full-blown panic.

"So much for that relaxing we talked about," Lee muttered.

"This *is* me relaxing." Darius's response prompted the entire team's laughter, easing their tension.

After the initial shock, he was able to get everyone focused.

The team had discussed the designs, agreed on a few changes, debated the correct ratio of nylon and spandex for the fabric, and identified sources for all of the materials.

In a few days he'd have prototypes for each swimsuit.

The doorbell rang and he checked his watch. Nearly six thirty. Was it that lawyer with the paternity test results?

Darius made his way toward the front door, with its large central glass pane. He'd only seen the face of the man standing on the other side of the door once before, but he'd never forget it.

He hesitated a moment. His steps suddenly felt leaden, and his heart pounded inside his chest.

For the past two days, he'd kept himself preoccupied with work. He hadn't allowed himself to wonder about the man who'd been his biological father or his newly discovered half siblings. But staring at the man in front of him, bearing features similar to his own, he was no longer able to avoid his new reality.

Darius exhaled slowly, as he unlocked the door.

How am I supposed to greet a possible sibling I didn't know I had until two days ago?

"Yes?" Lame, but the best he could do on short notice.

The man stared at him, wide-eyed, for a beat without response. Perhaps he was silently cataloguing Darius's features, too. The man withdrew a hand from his pocket and extended it. "Hello, Darius. I'm Kellan Blackwood." They shook hands. "It would appear that we're brothers."

They were complete strangers. Yet, they shared DNA. Their handshake was awkward. Too much and not enough, all at once.

"It seems so." Darius slid his hands into his pockets and leaned against the doorframe. "But I guess the paternity test will tell the final story."

"True." Kellan nodded. "My father and I weren't close. Mostly because we agreed on very little, and the man could be an asshole," he said without apology. "But I knew him well enough to know he'd never have gone to the trouble of bringing you here if he wasn't already dead sure you were his son. I get the feeling that the paternity test was requested to erase any doubt in our minds."

An uncomfortable silence settled over them.

Finally, Darius spoke. "Would you like to come in for a minute? I haven't had a chance to order groceries, but a fruit basket came with the place."

"No worries." Kellan pulled a bottle of premium Scotch from the inside of his denim jacket. He handed it to Darius. "Brought you a housewarming gift."

Darius thanked the man with a wary smile.

Is Kellan simply being hospitable? Does he want to get to know his newfound brother? Or is he here to dissuade me from sticking around and staking a claim on the estate?

"Come in." He led Kellan to the sitting room that overlooked the patio and pool. Darius grabbed two tumblers and set one in front of each of them, pouring them each two fingers of Scotch.

He was more of an imported beer guy, but he had the feeling this was some kind of test. One he didn't plan to fail.

Once they were both seated with glasses in hand, the awkward silence settled over them again.

Kellan took a deep sip of his Scotch, then set his glass down. "Darius, my brother, sister and I wanted you to know that we have no plans to dispute your right to a share of the estate."

"Good to know." Darius set his glass down, too. "Though it doesn't much matter since the old man cut all of us out of the estate."

"Straightforward and to the point. I like you already." Kellan chuckled and took another sip from his glass. "Guess we both got that trait honest."

Darius chuckled, too, sipping a bit of his Scotch. He resisted the urge to cough. Instead, he cleared his throat and met his brother's gaze. "Our father... What was he like?"

Kellan frowned. There was anger in his expression, but also pain. Maybe even a hint of guilt.

"A few months ago, I would've simply described him as an asshole. That's how I saw him most of my life."

"And now?"

"I still say he was an asshole, but he was a complicated one. He apparently had more depth than any of us gave him credit for. Too bad he didn't show any of us that side of himself while he was alive." Kellan drained the remainder of his glass. "Maybe then the old man wouldn't have died alone."

Kellan blamed their father's sad demise on the old man's gruff disposition. Still, there was the clear ring of guilt in his brother's tone and tortured expression. Darius didn't need to know the man well to recognize it.

It was the same guilt he felt regarding his mother and stepfather. They'd kept the truth from him, and he had every right to be angry. Yet, he'd begun to feel a deep sense of guilt about the distance he'd created between them.

"What shifted your opinion about him?" Darius needed to know there had been some good in the man who'd given him life.

Kellan's frown deepened. "I'm hungry," he declared suddenly. "Have you eaten yet?"

He'd evidently touched a nerve. So he wouldn't press the man.

"No." Darius shook his head. "Now that you mention it, I'm starving."

"There's this great little diner in town." Kellan stood.

"Royal Diner." Darius nodded. "Do they deliver? This isn't a conversation I'd like to have in public. In fact, I'm not ready to talk about any of this outside of…" The word caught in his throat.

"The family?" One edge of Kellan's mouth curved. "I should've considered that. I'll request delivery."

Kellan ordered himself a steak, though he confessed to having already eaten a light dinner earlier with Irina, his new bride. Darius requested the same meal he'd had the day before.

"Anything else?" Kellan asked. "Dinner's on me."

A light went on in the house next door and Audra walked past one of the downstairs windows.

Darius sighed, turning to Kellan. "I hear they make a really good Cobb salad."

Despite the initial awkwardness, Darius enjoyed getting to know Kellan, and through him, the rest of his newfound family. He couldn't help laughing at Kellan's tales of his and Vaughn's misadventures as boys. And he'd been moved by sweet stories about Sophie who'd been precocious, but sheltered, as a child.

"She's getting married." Kellan smiled fondly as he stared into his glass of Scotch after he'd finished his meal. "I'm nine years older than Sophie, so I took the job of looking out for her seriously. Sometimes I feel more like her father than her brother." Lines around his eyes crinkled. "I can't believe she's getting married. Then again, I can't believe I'm married again and that we're expecting a baby."

Darius had met this man a few hours ago. Had learned of his existence just yesterday. Yet, he was genuinely happy for him.

There was a natural kinship between them. A connection he hadn't felt with anyone else.

It was comforting, yet unnerving.

A splash in the pool snagged both men's attention.

Kellan stood abruptly. "Sorry. Didn't realize you had company."

Darius stood, too. "That's my neighbor. She's working on a project for your... I mean, *our* sister. The house next door doesn't have a pool, so Sophie told her she could use this one." He shrugged. "Didn't see the harm in allowing her to continue."

Kellan's mouth curved in a sly grin. "Must be quite a hardship to have a beautiful woman traipsing through your backyard in a swimsuit."

"How'd you know she's beautiful?" Darius eyed his brother suspiciously.

"The expression on your face said it all." Kellan chuckled. "You've got a thing for this woman."

"She also happens to be my ex," Darius confessed. "You can't imagine how shocked I was to see her here."

"Hmm… Is that right?" Kellan furrowed his brows. He picked up his empty to-go containers and cleaned his space. "Well, I've kept you long enough. I'd better check on my wife. She's been exhausted and sleeping a lot the past few weeks."

"I imagine it's tough work growing a human being." Darius walked Kellan to the front door. He extended a hand to his half brother. "Thank you for coming by, Kellan. It was good to meet you."

"Same." Kellan grinned as he shook Darius's hand. "This Saturday, we're volunteering at the Texas Cattleman's Club after the recent wildfires. The organization is important to our family, and we're all members. Sophie's a designer, so fixing the clubhouse back up has become her special project. Vaughn, Sophie and her fiancé, Nigel, will all be there. If you have the time, you should join us. We could use the help, and you'll be able to meet the rest of the family."

"Won't it be awkward if I'm there with all of you, since I'm not ready to make our relationship public?"

"You're a stranger here on business. That's all anyone needs to know." Kellan shrugged. "I'll make sure Sophie and Vaughn know you want to keep this under wraps for now. We've had longer to sit with the idea than you have. I'm sure you must be overwhelmed by all of this."

He was.

"Thanks for understanding. And, if I can manage it, I'll help out on Saturday."

Kellan clapped a hand on his shoulder. "Great. Hope to see you then. If you need anything in the meantime…" He retrieved his wallet from his back pocket and handed Darius a business card. "Call my cell number anytime, day or night."

"Will do." Darius studied the card. Kellan was a Nashville-based real estate developer.

He gave Kellan one of his business cards, then cleared his throat. The words he'd needed to say all night lay at the back of his tongue, like heavy, immovable stones.

"About this whole thing... I'm sorry. I realize how hard it must be to learn that your father was unfaithful to your mother. I wouldn't blame any of you for being upset by me being here."

"I appreciate the thought." Kellan winced, almost imperceptibly. "But you're not to blame. We knew who our father was. Unfortunately, my mother did, too." He flashed a pained smile. "None of that matters anymore. You're family now."

Darius wished his brother a good night and closed the door behind him. A deep sense of relief alleviated the heaviness in his chest.

He returned to the darkened room overlooking the pool and stood quietly, watching Audra's arms slice through the water as she swam laps.

Seeing Audra again, after all of these years, had brought all those feelings to the surface that he'd buried so deeply when he'd walked away from her.

It'd been the right decision, but one he'd often regretted.

Audra was an amazing woman. Devastatingly sexy, stunningly beautiful and smart as a whip. She had a goofy sense of humor most people wouldn't expect of the product of two legendary families, deeply entrenched in business and politics. Regardless of what was happening in his life, she'd always been able to make him laugh.

She was a fellow creative who understood the mania of needing to work through the night on a project. Or the need to wake up at three in the morning to sketch out a design that came to him in his sleep.

Despite her family's wealth, Audra never came off as spoiled or pampered. She was the quintessential girl next door. Her house just happened to be a sprawling, multimillion-dollar mansion.

Go back to the office. You've got a ton of work to do.

He hadn't been honest with Audra back then, nor was he prepared to tell her everything now. He'd hurt her when he'd ended their relationship. He wouldn't hurt her again.

But Audra was like the sun. Her gravitational pull hauled him into her orbit. He was inescapably drawn to her then and now. And with everything else going on in his life, he didn't have the strength to resist her pull.

He grabbed the Cobb salad he'd put in the fridge and made his way to the backyard.

Audra was in the middle of her tenth lap when she noticed Darius approaching.

She gripped the edge of the pool and slid her goggles on top of her head. "Hi."

He sat on the edge of the lounge chair beside the one that held her things. "Hey."

She made her way to the stainless steel ladder, and Darius extended his open palm, pulling her up. Then he handed her one of her towels.

"Thanks." Audra dried her face and dripping wet hair before wrapping the other towel around her body. His expression was largely unreadable, but there was clearly *something* he wanted to say. "Have you changed your mind about me using the pool?"

"No, of course not. It's just that it's late and—"

"Sorry, I don't usually swim this late, but I've been reworking a client design and I got so absorbed in the project that time got away from me."

"Audra." Darius placed a hand on her arm. "You're fine. Stay out here all night, if you'd like. I don't care. I just... I had dinner delivered from the Royal Diner. I thought I'd try the Cobb salad you recommended, but I honestly couldn't eat another bite. I thought you might like it."

He nodded toward the bag he'd set on a small table between the lounge chairs. "Have you eaten?"

"No. I planned to throw something together after my laps."

"Well, now you won't have to. If you want it, that is." Darius shoved his hands in his pockets.

"Sure." She shrugged. "Thanks."

Silence, as thick and heavy as the brick wall that separated their yards, hung between them in the chilly night air. The weight of their unspoken words sent a shiver down her spine and made her belly tense.

Darius's cell phone rang, and she could swear he sighed in relief. He pulled it from his pocket and checked the caller ID. Darius groaned, then flashed an apologetic smile.

"I'd better take this." He stared at her a moment longer. "Good night, Audra."

He strode away, answering the call.

Audra released a long, slow breath as Darius walked away.

There were a million reasons she shouldn't be eye-

ing his perfect ass and broad shoulders, remembering
how it felt to lie in his arms.

Audra tightened the towel wrapped around her to
ward off the chilly, night air. But the shiver running
up her spine stemmed from the vivid, visceral memories of how amazing it had felt when Darius kissed her.
Made love to her.

She'd never been with anyone like him. The sex had
been incredible, yes. But it had been so much more than
that. No one had ever made her feel the way Darius had.
Like she was the center of his universe. Not her famous
family or her bank account. Just her.

She hadn't had that feeling before or since. Sometimes, she wondered if she'd ever feel that way again.

But clearly, it had all been an act. If she'd meant half
as much to him as he had to her, he'd never have walked
away. And he wouldn't have lied to her about something
as important as his family.

Audra nibbled on her lower lip. Her heart felt heavy
and her gut twisted in a knot. She should be glad Darius hadn't invited her inside.

So why do I wish he had?

She grabbed her things, slipped on her sandals and
picked up the bag from the Royal Diner. Then she headed
toward the iron gate that separated the properties.

Audra couldn't help glancing at the office window
where Darius was on the phone, pacing.

Two days ago, she was sure she was over Darius.
Now she couldn't help wondering if she would ever
truly be over him.

Seven

It was just after nine on Saturday morning and Darius had already been up for a couple of hours. He stared at the magnetic whiteboard he'd purchased the previous day.

He'd printed out sketches of the garments in Thr3d's fall collection and secured them to the whiteboard with colorful magnets. Darius moved the pieces around several times, pairing items that could be worn together. He rearranged the order of the runway lineup to best convey his vision of Thr3d to the fashion buyers and the audience.

Thr3d produced functional, high-performance, technology-friendly athletic wear. The hip, colorful vibe allowed wearers to express themselves. The range of sizes were inclusive. The basic collection was priced to be accessible, while the premier collection offered high-end sportswear.

He'd been so intent on the task that he'd only been minimally distracted by Audra's morning swim.

A runway show at LA Fashion Week was huge for Thr3d. This show could get Thr3d into more retail spaces and raise brand awareness among consumers and social influencers around the world. The pressure to put on a perfect show weighed on his shoulders like a boulder.

He couldn't get this wrong. Too much was riding on it. So he wouldn't allow deceased, absentee fathers, newfound siblings or resurfacing exes to divert him from the vision he'd been working toward for the past five years. The success he'd craved his entire life.

He needed to keep his mind in motion and thoughts of Audra out of his head.

The doorbell rang. Part of him hoped it was Audra dropping by. But she'd obviously moved on, as he'd hoped she would. Still, after seeing her the past few days, he couldn't help reminiscing about their past.

He cared for Audra. Wanted her to be happy. But the thought of her being happy with some other guy killed him inside.

The bell rang again, shaking him from his daze. He approached the door and saw a familiar figure on the other side.

Kace LeBlanc. The lawyer.

The man was dressed in jeans and a T-shirt, rather than his expensive suit.

Darius opened the door. "Mr. LeBlanc. I assume you're here with news for me."

"Kace will do just fine." The man looked beyond him. "Would it be all right if I stepped inside to update you on the latest development?"

Darius gestured for the man to come inside. "Are you here to toss me out as an imposter?"

"Not at all." Kace handed Darius two envelopes. The larger one contained the scrapbook Buck had compiled with all of his accomplishments. The one Miranda had promised him once the DNA test proved that he was Buckley Blackwood's son. "You are indeed a legal heir of Buckley Blackwood, entitled to the same rights as his legitimate children."

The man's use of the word *legitimate* reignited the ugly feelings he'd struggled with for more than a decade. The feeling of not belonging anywhere. Not being wanted by his own father.

"And that entitles me to what, exactly?" Darius shrugged, setting both the envelopes on a nearby table without opening them. "A general 'fuck-you, son'? Blackwood has given me that my entire life. But at least he's been consistent. Seems the man treated all his children that way—*legitimate* or otherwise."

"I can understand why you'd see things that way." Kace folded his arms. "But your father cared for you— all of you—more than you know. Coming here wasn't a waste of your time, Darius. You've discovered that you have siblings, whom you seem to have a lot in common with."

"Such as?" Darius stared at the man.

"You're all good people and successful entrepreneurs. And you're all working through your grief over the loss of your father." The man's expression was kind.

"How could I possibly grieve for a man I never knew?" Darius's voice was strangled. His neck and shoulders tensed as he clenched his fists at his sides.

"I suppose you've been grieving, in a way, from the

moment you learned Will Pratt wasn't your biological father."

Heat flared in Darius's face. He was still angry with his mother and Will, but he wouldn't allow anyone else to disparage them.

"You don't know anything about my relationship with Will Pratt," he said, quietly seething beneath his calm facade. "He's ten times the father Buckley Blackwood ever was."

The truth of that statement struck him like an aluminum bat to the back of his head.

William Pratt had been a father to him by choice—in name and deed. The man deserved credit for that. Credit Darius hadn't given him.

"I'm sure, and I didn't mean to offend you." The two men stood in momentary silence before Kace spoke again. "Now that you know the truth, what's next for you, Darius?"

"Getting to know my brothers and sister, I suppose." Darius shrugged. "Then I'll decide whether or not to contest the will."

"Then I guess we'll be seeing you around town," Kace said. "In fact, several of us are volunteering at the Texas Cattleman's Club today. The clubhouse means a lot to folks in Royal, and your siblings will be there. This project is Sophie's baby."

"Shit," Darius muttered, checking his watch. "That's today? Kellan asked if I'd help."

"Royal Diner is providing breakfast. I'm headed to the TCC clubhouse now, if you need a lift into town."

Darius turned the idea over in his head.

Now that he was officially a Blackwood, he felt a pressing need to get to know his siblings. His meeting with Kellan had gone well. But that didn't guarantee things would go as smoothly with Sophie and Vaughn.

Hell, for all he knew, the meeting with Kellan was just a pretense to make him let down his guard. Maybe Kellan just wanted to gain his trust so he could convince him to pack his things and leave town.

"Darius." Kace sounded apologetic as he broke into his thoughts. "Can I give you a ride to the clubhouse?" He patted his belly. "I don't mind telling you I'm starving."

"Give me five minutes?"

Kace nodded. "I'll give you ten."

Darius went to the master bedroom and changed into a Thr3d T-shirt, cargo pants and sneakers. Then he inhaled a deep breath, mentally preparing himself to spend the day getting to know his half siblings without revealing his parentage to anyone else in town.

"Darius." Kellan approached him with a wide smile. "Glad you made it."

Darius shook his brother's hand. "Kace came over earlier with some news. He reminded me about volunteering today."

"So your paternity has been confirmed?" Kellan lowered his voice.

"I'm definitely a Blackwood."

"It was pretty clear to me the moment I met you. You've got a lot of the family features."

Darius scanned the room. *Will anyone else notice our physical similarities?*

"I talked to Sophie and Vaughn. We respect your decision to keep the news quiet while you process all of this," Kellan assured him.

"I appreciate that. I'd like to talk to my mother and

stepfather before the news goes public. My relationship with them hasn't been the best these past few years." He felt the need to justify his decision. "But they deserve a conversation in person before word gets out."

"Of course." Kellan nodded. "Let me show you around and introduce you to some of the folks in—"

"Oh my God. Darius, you came."

They both turned to the sweet voice that trembled with emotion. He recognized his half sister, Sophie, from the picture Kace had shown him and the two hours of her lifestyle show webisodes he'd watched after Googling her. She was a gorgeous, full-figured woman with a smile as bright as the sun. Her brown eyes shone with tears.

She wiped at them and forced a laugh. "I mean, it's kind of you to volunteer this morning. For the club and for me. This is where I hope to have my wedding." She paused, studying his face. She lowered her voice to just above a whisper. "Is it all right if I hug you?"

His mouth spread in an involuntary grin and his eyes burned with emotion. Darius nodded. "I'd like that."

Sophie wrapped her arms around him and squeezed tight. She held on to him, and he let her. Her response was so sincere. He forced himself not to obsess over the conclusions other people might jump to about them.

Instead, he was grateful for her warm reception.

He was an older brother now. His sister seemed to need this moment of connection, and he already felt an instinctive protectiveness toward her.

He'd been an only child, so this was a new experience for him. But he enjoyed this unfamiliar sense of belonging.

He was lucky. Things could've gone much differently. He was keenly aware of that.

"I'm sorry." Sophie released him, dabbing at her eyes. "I know we're keeping this on the low for now."

"It's okay." Darius smiled. "Congratulations on your engagement."

"Thank you." She beamed, then lowered her voice. "Please tell me you'll come to the wedding. No one has to know you're my brother, if that's what you'd prefer. But it would mean a lot to me if you came."

"If there are no conflicts with my schedule, I promise I'll be there."

"Good." Sophie seemed satisfied with his response. "Have you eaten? If not, you have to grab a breakfast sandwich and some coffee or juice. Then I'll introduce you to some of the folks in town. Let me go find Nigel. He's probably on the phone somewhere." Sophie wandered off to locate her fiancé.

"Welcome to the family." Kellan chuckled, his voice low.

"Is Vaughn here?" Darius asked.

Kellan frowned and sipped his coffee. "He sent a couple of his ranch hands instead." Kellan nodded toward two men standing in the corner nibbling on breakfast sandwiches.

"Maybe he wasn't up for meeting me," Darius said without resentment. It made sense that at least one of the three wouldn't be eager to welcome him to the family.

"Vaughn lives in Fort Worth, and he doesn't darken the town's doorstep, if he can avoid it. He wants nothing to do with our father, dead or alive."

Perhaps that was why Vaughn wasn't contesting the

estate. He didn't want any part of the painful memories that went along with it.

Seems he was the lucky one to never have known Buckley Blackwood.

"I get it." Darius shrugged as they walked toward the breakfast buffet setup. "I didn't take the revelation that Will wasn't my biological father very well. I didn't feel I could trust them anymore. Our relationship hasn't been the same since."

"I can appreciate how difficult that must've been for you. But I wouldn't be surprised if your parents were obligated to keep your paternity to themselves. That's the way my father operated. So I wouldn't be too hard on them. Maybe they didn't have much choice." Kellan patted his shoulder. "I see someone I need to speak with, but I'll be back in a minute."

Darius stood there as Kellan walked away. He hadn't considered the possibility that there was a viable reason his mother hadn't disclosed his bio father's name.

Had Buck forced his parents to keep his secret in exchange for the financial support that had made it possible for him to attend schools like Harvard?

It was a secret the old man probably would've done just about anything to keep.

Maybe Kellan was right. Maybe he'd been too hard on them.

"Darius. What are you doing here?" Audra stared at him, her eyes wide.

She looked adorable in a pair of gray, cropped cargo pants and a long-sleeve white T-shirt. A heart-shaped gold locket, which matched the color and shape of her nose ring, dragged his attention to the deep vee of her shirt.

"A few of the locals invited me to volunteer. I decided I could use the mental break." His gaze shifted from hers.

A deep ache in his gut nagged at him for hiding his connection to the Blackwoods from Audra. But the runway show was just a few weeks away. He wouldn't risk the story about the CEO of Thr3d being the "bastard child" of the late Buckley Blackwood getting out and overshadowing the show. He didn't believe Audra would intentionally sabotage him. But what if someone overheard them or she told the wrong person?

Everything has to be perfect for this show.

It wasn't a chance he could afford to take. "I figured I'd help out for a few hours. How about you?"

"Sophie…my client—" Audra nodded in Sophie's direction "—asked me to help. Besides, several members of the bridal party are here. This gives me the chance to get to know them as I try to finalize the designs for their custom jewelry gifts."

"Makes perfect sense." He nodded.

They stood together in awkward silence. Close enough that he could feel the heat radiating from her smooth, toasted-brown skin and smell the sweet citrus scent wafting from her hair. Finally, Darius couldn't take the vivid images of them together—him touching her, kissing her, making love to her—that his brain conjured in the absence of words.

"Have you eaten breakfast yet?" he asked, abruptly.

"I haven't, and I'm starving. I was about to grab a sandwich, if you'd care to join me."

"Sure." Audra followed him toward the bar where the food was set up. "And thank you for the salad the other night. It was thoughtful of you."

"For you, Audra? Anything."

Eight

Resentment bubbled up in Audra's chest and her hands clenched at her side.

Liar.

How dare he utter those words to her? If he'd truly do anything for her, he wouldn't have lied about his parents who were still very much alive. And he would've been honest about whatever it was that had prompted him to end their relationship.

"Darius, I want you to meet my fiancé, Nigel Townshend," Sophie was saying as she approached him. When Sophie caught sight of her behind Darius, her eyes widened. "Audra, I didn't realize you were here."

"I arrived five minutes ago." Audra folded her arms. "I thought you didn't know Darius."

"We met this morning," Sophie said quickly. "I wanted him to meet Nigel."

"Hello, Darius." Nigel extended his hand. "I'm Nigel Townshend, Sophie's fiancé. I run the *Secret Lives of NYC Ex-Wives*."

"Good to meet you." Darius shook Nigel's hand.

"Coffee?" Audra grabbed a mug and pulled the lever on the stainless steel coffee urn, dispensing the hot, black, aromatic liquid.

"Please," Darius said. "Black with—"

"Two sugars," she completed his sentence without thought.

They'd studied together over coffee. First at a coffee shop on campus. Eventually at her apartment the morning after he'd stayed over for breakfast…and more.

"Yes. Thank you." There was something warm and familiar in Darius's gaze that filled her chest with heat and made her belly flutter.

Audra returned her attention to the coffee station where she made his cup, then her own. By the time she'd grabbed a Danish for herself and rejoined the conversation, Sophie was asking Darius about his upcoming runway show at LA Fashion Week.

"I try to get out to the show whenever I can," Sophie said. "But with all of the preparations still to be made for the wedding… I don't know if I'll make it this year."

"If you can swing it, I hope you'll come. Just let me know and I'll reserve VIP passes for both of you." Darius sipped his coffee.

A generous offer to make to strangers.

But then, Sophie was a social influencer with an ever-popular lifestyle channel on YouTube and Nigel was a powerful television exec. It paid to have high-powered friends like that.

"You'll be attending the event, too, won't you, Audra?" Sophie asked excitedly.

"I'm supplying the jewelry for a couple of the designers," Audra confirmed.

It was a lucrative partnership. The design houses didn't purchase her jewelry for their runway shows. She loaned them the pieces. But she cleared millions of dollars in jewelry sales based on the free publicity.

"Great. Maybe we can get together in LA after your shows and celebrate." Sophie's gaze went from Darius's face to hers.

Neither of them responded right away.

"That would be great," Darius said, finally, then added, "If that's something Audra would want."

"Sure. If I can fit it into my schedule." Audra shrugged, then nibbled on the last of her Danish. "Now, who is it that I'm supposed to see about a volunteer assignment?"

"Ah...fresh blood." A strikingly handsome man with intense green eyes joined them.

"Ryan Bateman, meet Audra Lee Covington. She's in town to design some custom jewelry pieces for my wedding. And this is Darius Taylor-Pratt, who is here on business with Miranda Dupree. He's the founder and CEO of the athletic wear company, Thr3d." Sophie almost sounded proud of Darius.

"I'm a fan of your men's sportswear." Ryan tugged on the black shirt he was wearing. "And the Neapolitan engagement ring I got my wife was one of your limited edition pieces." He nodded toward Audra. "It's a stunning ring."

"Where is Tessa?" Sophie asked.

"Sophie! How are you?" A beautiful, brown-skinned

woman with long, curly hair approached them. Her generous hips and full figure reminded Audra a lot of Sophie's as the two women hugged.

"Congratulations on your engagement. This must be your fiancé." Tessa shook Nigel's hand. "I've seen your crew around town."

"I trust that they aren't causing you too much trouble." Nigel's eyes sparkled.

Sophie introduced Tessa to Darius and then to her. Tessa was delighted to meet the designer of her engagement ring, and Audra was touched by the woman's heartfelt appreciation.

After five years of designing her own jewelry collections, it still moved her when a client gushed over one of her creations.

"I'm honored that you love it so much," Audra said.

"And I'm honored to meet you." A handsome man with the same nearly glowing, light brown eyes as Tessa's suddenly appeared. He shook her hand, staring at her as if he were mesmerized. "I'm Tessa's brother, Tripp Noble."

I bet you are a trip.

"Audra Lee Covington." She tugged her hand from his. "Good to meet you, Tripp."

She glanced over at Darius. His nostrils flared, and he looked like he wanted to toss Tripp outside, Jazzy Jeff style.

"Looks like we'll be teamed up." Tripp smirked.

"Darius and Audra are already teamed up," Sophie pinned Tripp with a narrowed gaze. "They dated back in grad school."

Tripp gave Sophie a subtle shrug.

"Milan!" Sophie waved another woman over. "You're just in time. Tripp needs a partner."

"Wait…what?" Milan narrowed her gaze at Tripp. He smiled sheepishly.

There was a story there if ever Audra had seen one.

Sophie introduced Milan Valez, a professional makeup artist who worked at the local salon and spa PURE.

"Our assignment is to replant the vegetation and to clean up the outdoor furniture that was salvaged by moving it offsite." Sophie reviewed a clipboard. "We'll be working throughout the outdoor space in teams of two, so…" She surveyed everyone gathered. "That's Ryan and Tess, Tripp and Milan, Darius and Audra, me and Nigel, Kace and…"

"Good morning, Lulu," Nigel greeted a woman Audra recognized as Lulu Shepard, one of the stars of the *Secret Lives of NYC Ex-Wives* show.

"Good morning, everyone." The woman raked her fingernails through her glossy black hair. Her gorgeous, dark brown skin practically glowed. She wore moto-style Balmain skinny jeans in a gray wash, a high-end, celebrity-brand graphic T-shirt that proclaimed *I'm Not Bossy, I'm a Boss* and a pair of black Prada riding boots. Not the kind of gear one typically wore for a dirty job like gardening or cleaning. But still, she looked amazing.

When Lulu's eyes met Kace's, there was a definite spark between the two. The man shifted his gaze.

Another man being mysterious about his feelings.

"I'm not sure where I should be right now." Lulu shrugged.

"Perfect. Because Kace needs a partner," Sophie

said. "And Kellan, would you float between projects and give folks a hand wherever needed?"

"Sure, sis." Kellan held up his cup of coffee.

"I'm surprised you didn't object to Sophie teaming us up." Darius spoke in a hushed tone as they trailed Ryan and Tessa to the outdoor space.

"You did buy me dinner last night." She shrugged. "Wait… Did you ask Sophie to team us up?"

"Me?" His dark eyes went wide. There was definitely something up with him today. Not that he owed her an explanation. "No, I thought maybe you did. You obviously told her about our history."

"I wasn't gossiping about us, if that's what you're thinking." Audra's cheeks heated and her heart beat faster. "I mentioned that I'd run into my ex in town. Sophie asked who, and I told her. End of story. Maybe she thought we'd be comfortable working together because we already know each other."

"Well, I'm glad we're working together," he said. "It'll be nice to catch up."

Audra wasn't sure she agreed.

But she could do this. She could let go of her resentment and work with Darius. All she had to do was pretend her heart wasn't still tender over their breakup. And ignore the attraction that made her belly do flips whenever his gaze met hers.

Lulu stood on the TCC pool deck where she and Kace had been assigned to clean all of the furniture that had been stored offsite, beyond the fire's reach, but had still sustained some smoke damage.

She realized that most folks there probably believed she was volunteering simply to get prime footage for their reality show. But she'd asked the camera crew—currently following Rafaela and a few of the other women from the show who were there volunteering, too—to leave her out of any footage filmed that day. She'd come here for one reason: she wanted to help.

The devastation she'd seen, caused by the wildfires, had broken her heart. And despite what some people might think, she did in fact have a heart. A huge one she worked hard to hide behind her bubbly, playful, nothing-gets-to-me persona.

A woman in television had to be tough. A woman of color doubly so.

It was the façade she'd needed to adopt to protect her heart from the humiliation of her former football player ex-husband, Roderick Evans, replacing her with a pop star who'd had her own show on a kids' television network just a few years earlier.

And it was that bubbly, playful persona that garnered the attention of Nigel Townshend and the other execs when they were putting together their new reality show. The show was looking for a funny, wise-cracking character who never let anything faze her. Lulu's painstakingly procured persona fit the bill.

Her vulnerabilities she kept carefully tucked away.

"Everything okay?" Kace touched her arm, startling her. She could feel his warm, sweet breath on her ear.

Did anyone else notice the intimate gesture?

"I'm fine." Lulu withdrew her arm and stepped backward, nearly tripping over a small table.

Kace steadied her. His warm brown eyes glinted in the sunlight as they focused on hers, hidden behind a pair of Dolce & Gabbana sunglasses.

"Lu, are you sure you're okay?" he whispered.

"Of course." Lulu looked around. Fortunately, the camera crew was following Rafaela.

She stepped away from him, carefully this time, and picked up the two aprons, handing one to Kace.

"Why are we the only ones wearing aprons?" he asked, one brow raised. "Are they afraid you'll ruin your designer jeans and T-shirt?" His voice had a light, teasing tone, rather than the harsh one they'd used with each other when they'd met a few months ago.

"I suspect it's because we're the only ones working with bleach." She sniffed the scent rising from one of the buckets to confirm her suspicions.

"Noted." Kace was a man of few words when he wasn't being paid by the hour as a lawyer for his wealthy clientele. Clients like the obscenely rich, dead ex-husband of Lulu's costar Miranda Dupree.

Lulu looped the apron over her head and reached behind her to tie the strings.

"Let me get that," Kace offered, dropping his apron back onto the nearby chair. He took the apron strings from her hand and tied them at her back before her brain could register any objection.

"There." Kace secured the strings and stepped back, his eyes slowly gliding over her.

She was fully dressed. So why did she feel so naked beneath his gaze?

It was as if Kace could see to the very core of her being. Beyond the fronting, assumed persona, and any of the other bullshit she employed that served as a moat, drawbridge and flaming arrows to protect the one thing she was determined never to expose again: her heart.

Then, of course, there was the fact that he had, in reality, seen her naked.

Geez. What was with her? And why couldn't she resist this man?

Kace LeBlanc projected a "Just the facts, ma'am," by-the-book, stick-up-his-ass image to the world. But beneath that rigid exterior lay sensitivity and insight. Compassion. And an extremely passionate lover. All of which made her want him even more. But they were so different. Any attempt at a real relationship between them would surely end in disaster.

Yet, they had failed spectacularly at staying away from each other.

Did Sophie pick up on that vibe? Is that why she assigned us to work together?

They were getting sloppy with this whole undercover hookup thing. And the longer this went on, the more inconspicuous they were becoming.

"You're staring again." A barely perceptible smile turned up one edge of his sensual mouth.

"You've got soot on your cheek," she said, reaching up to wipe it away with her thumb.

"Must've transferred from the furniture when I picked up this apron." He positioned the garment over his clothing.

"Here, I've got it." Lulu stepped behind him and returned the favor by tying his apron. Then she slipped gloves on over her short but manicured fingernails. "Ready to get started?"

"You bet." Kace picked up a pair of gloves and put them on, too. "The quicker we get this done, the sooner I can get you back to my place." He leaned closer, whispering that last part in her ear.

A shiver ran down her spine.

"And just what makes you think I have any intention of going to your place?" She propped a hand on her hip. "I'm going to be grimy and dirty, and I'll need a shower and a change of clothes."

"I just happen to have a shower at my place," he said with a sarcastic grin. "And as for clothing, you're not going to need those for what I've got planned."

Damn.

Kace LeBlanc was getting more comfortable revealing glimpses of his softer, more relaxed self to her. The side of himself he didn't seem comfortable showing the rest of the world. Even in a white apron, scruffy casual clothing and a pair of rubber gloves, she couldn't help being attracted to him.

Her nipples grew taut and there was a steady pulse between her thighs, just thinking of all the ways he'd sated her body. Even just his kiss possessed the power to set her entire body on fire and leave her stunned, babbling nonsense.

It felt good to have a man so damn willing to satisfy her every need. But it was terrifying, too.

Mediocre lovers were easy to walk away from.

But a man who had brains, an incredible body and a sense of compassion… That combination was damned hard to leave behind.

"To be determined" was the only comeback she could manage.

Yep, he was definitely fucking with her head. She was the Queen of Quips. When had she ever been speechless?

"I'll take this bucket with the bleach solution." Kace stooped to pick up the bucket. "Wouldn't want you to get bleach spots on all that fancy gear you're wearing."

"These were supplied by the show's wardrobe department," she replied, picking up her bucket and sitting it beside a chair. "Besides, if I get bleach spots on these jeans, it'll make them look distressed, which is totally on trend this season."

Kace narrowed his gaze at her, shook his head and chuckled. He pulled out the scrub brush and went to work.

Lulu couldn't help smiling to herself as she picked up her soft brush and started to scrub a chair nearby.

Nine

After a grueling day working in the gardens at the Texas Cattleman's Club, Audra was tired and dirty, and her muscles ached.

She wanted nothing more than a long, hot, relaxing bubble bath with the jets turned up to full blast.

Despite the exhaustion and soreness, she'd enjoyed the day immensely. It'd been fun getting to know Sophie and her friends. And as much as she hated to admit it, she'd enjoyed working with Darius.

He'd been thoughtful—making sure she had water, coffee and snacks throughout the day. He'd been fiercely protective—worrying that she'd hurt herself using some of the equipment. And he'd been sweet and supportive when she'd chattered on, bouncing ideas off of him about a new limited edition collection of jewelry she was putting together.

It reminded her of how well matched they'd always been. Like two pieces of a puzzle. Which only made it more painful that he'd lied to her and then given up on their relationship without the decency of leveling with her about why.

She'd been determined to keep their interactions friendly and platonic. But she couldn't help that her wandering eyes were repeatedly drawn to the curve of his ass and the way his broad chest and shoulders expanded the material of his fitted shirt.

Nor could she help the naughty thoughts that ran rampant through her head as she remembered the feel of his body and wondered how much it had changed.

"Thanks for coming, Audra." Sophie squeezed her hand. "You, too, Darius."

"Of course." He nodded. "It was a pleasure to meet you all." He surveyed the main room of the clubhouse where people laughed and talked after a hard day's work. "I can see why everyone seems to love this town so much."

"Then maybe you'll stick around after your business with Miranda is done." Sophie grinned. "By the way, Kace had to leave, and he mentioned that he gave you a ride here. I imagine you'll need a ride back."

"I'm calling a car service." He held up his phone, the app already open.

"That's silly," Audra objected. "You're staying right next door to me. I'll give you a ride."

"Perfect." Sophie beamed. "Audra, I'll call you later. And Darius, I guess I'll be seeing you around town."

They said their good-nights to Sophie and then headed toward the parking lot.

"I didn't want to assume you were going straight home. Nor do I want to impose on you," Darius said.

"Where else would I possibly go looking like I've been making mud pies all day?" She stopped and turned toward him.

He broke into laughter, a sound she realized she'd missed. The corner of his mouth curved in a slow smile. "You might be a little dirty, Audra. That doesn't change the fact that you're a head turner. It certainly didn't keep your new friend Tripp from buzzing around you all day."

"Jealous?" She folded her arms, enjoying the tortured look on Darius's face.

"Of course not." His cheeks turned bright red and he cleared his throat. "What right do I have to be jealous of Tripp or any other man who takes an interest in you?"

Not the response she was hoping for—especially since it was complete bullshit. He'd practically stumbled over a garden hoe earlier, trying to get close enough to hear the conversation she'd been having with Tripp, an unabashed flirt.

"It was just an observation." Darius glanced at her convertible, quickly changing the subject. "Nice ride, but we're going to get your leather seats dirty."

"I've got it covered."

She popped the trunk and took out an old blanket she kept in the car, just in case.

"I should've known you would've come prepared." He chuckled.

Audra opened the door and started spreading the blanket on her side. It was long enough to cover Darius's seat, too, while leaving their seat belts and the central panel with the gearshift exposed.

They got buckled in and she headed toward their rental homes, riding mostly in silence.

"You're not actually interested in that guy, are you?" Darius asked suddenly,

The question took her by surprise.

"Like you said, what right do you have to be concerned about who I'm interested in?" She maintained her forward gaze.

"None." Darius heaved a sigh. "But that doesn't mean I'm not concerned about you, Audra. I want the best for you. I always have."

"And who made you the determiner of what's best for me?" She glanced at him briefly before returning her eyes to the road. "Tripp is a perfectly nice guy, from a perfectly nice family. He's a fourth-generation rancher, and his parents recently turned the business over to him."

"So he's wealthy and from a *good*—" he used air quotes "—family. Does that mean he can't be a creep? In my experience, that's the dude with the murder room in his basement."

"You have experience with that, do you?" She rolled her eyes as she turned into the Pine Valley community and the guards waved them through the gates. "Well, in my experience, one guy is just as untrustworthy as the next. It's just a matter of playing the odds and hoping you win."

"You deserve better, Audra. Better than Tripp or me." Darius's voice was faint. Almost as if he'd said the words to himself and she just happened to overhear them.

"Am I supposed to be flattered that you're so concerned about my well-being that you've appointed yourself the judge of who is good enough for me and who isn't?" Her voice was suddenly tense. She clutched the steering wheel as she swung into the driveway of her rental and parked in the attached garage.

Audra turned off the engine and turned to face him. "If you'd really cared, you would've stuck around. Or at least been honest about why you left."

Darius grimaced. He opened his mouth to speak, then shut it again.

Figures.

"It doesn't really matter now, does it?" It hurt that he wouldn't even put in the effort to make a good excuse. Or, heaven forbid, finally tell her the truth. "Good night, Darius."

She stepped out of the car and shut the door much harder than she'd intended to.

Darius climbed out of the car, too. He removed the blanket from her leather seats and folded it.

"Despite how the day ended, I enjoyed working with you today, Audra."

"Same," she murmured begrudgingly.

He handed the blanket to her. "Thanks for the ride. Good night."

Darius walked out of the garage and across the lawn that separated their driveways.

Audra punched the button and watched as the garage door lowered, her eyes burning with tears.

Lulu opened the door of her hotel room at the Bellamy and looked either way. The hallway was clear of her costars, the camera crew and the numerous people who worked behind the scenes of the show.

She slipped out of the door, closing it behind her and

hurrying to the elevator, relieved to make it to the lobby without encountering any of the show's staff.

She headed away from the main entrance, toward an obscure side entrance where her ride service was waiting.

Lulu adjusted her shades and tugged the sloppy beanie hat further down on her head as she slipped into the back seat of the car.

When the car dropped her off at the requested address, she got out, propped her leather backpack on her shoulder and tipped the man generously. When he drove away, she walked a few doors down to her actual destination.

Lulu climbed the stairs to the front door of the brick home painted beige. The fabric awning, shutters and wide front door were dark green, complementing the greenery in the landscaping.

Lulu sucked in a deep breath and rang the doorbell.

The door opened and Kace stood there staring at her. One side of his mouth curled in a sexy grin that made her want to climb him like a five-foot-eleven tree and have her way with him.

"About time you showed up." He swung the door open wider, allowing her to step inside.

"Don't get cocky, cowboy. Just because I'm here, it doesn't mean I'll stay." She stood along the wall, her arms folded as she surveyed the space. She'd been there before, but at the time she'd been too preoccupied with tearing off Kace's clothes to pay attention to the wallpaper and drapes.

"Yes, ma'am." He gave her a sly grin.

"And you did *not* know I'd come here."

He didn't acknowledge her objection. "The lasagna

will be done shortly. I was just about to heat up the dinner rolls."

He led her through the house into the formal dining room where he had two places set.

"You *did* expect me." Lulu turned to him in amazement.

"I certainly hoped you'd come." He shrugged, an almost sheepish smile on his handsome face as he raked his hands through his brown mop of curls, still damp from the shower. "Belief can be a powerful thing."

"My grandmother used to say that." She smiled faintly.

"A wise woman," Kace said as he took her backpack and jacket. He placed them in one chair and pulled out another for her.

"I'd prefer to help in the kitchen, if you don't mind." She inhaled the fresh, clean scent of his soap.

He led the way to the kitchen, and they chatted while she cut up vegetables for their salad.

"This is such a beautiful, charming old home." She glanced around the space. "When was it built?"

"Back in 1925. It belonged to my grandparents. My grandmother left it to me. I'm the only child of their only child," he said, "so the competition wasn't very stiff."

She laughed. "Did they do all of this updating to the place, too?"

The house was filled with character and original features like the marble fireplace hearth, hardwood floors and beautiful French doors. But it had lots of modern conveniences, too, like a beautiful kitchen island with seating and stainless steel appliances.

"No, that was all me. I started with the kitchen and I've been doing one room at a time until I'm finished."

"It's beautiful, and it's nothing at all like I would've expected your place to be. But for that matter, you're nothing at all like I would've expected, either."

He slipped one arm around her waist and cradled her cheek with the other hand. "Neither are you, Lulu Shepard." He pressed a soft, sweet kiss to her mouth.

Lulu wrapped her arms around his back, still slightly damp through his soft cotton T-shirt. She lifted onto her toes, trying to close the remaining gap between their heights in her three-inch heels.

There was something in Kace's kiss that sparked a fire within her and sent shivers down her spine. Her body instantly reacted to his touch. Her nipples beaded and she ached for him.

Kace backed her against a wall, his hands roaming over her curves as his kiss grew more demanding. Her heart thumped harder and her pulse raced as his tongue glided against hers and he gripped her bottom, pulling her body tighter against his hardened length.

"I don't think I have to tell you how much I want you," he whispered against her skin as he trailed kisses down her neck.

He grabbed the edge of her short knit dress and inched the hem up over her hips.

Suddenly, the oven's buzzer sounded.

Kace blew out a frustrated breath and pressed another kiss to her lips. "We'll finish this later."

Lulu could only manage a nod. She lowered the hem of her dress, her heart still racing and her chest heaving as she caught her breath.

Kace took the lasagna and rolls out of the oven and

took them to the table. She followed with the salad and bottle of wine.

They actually managed to make it through the meal—laughing, chatting and shamelessly flirting—before he took her to bed and made love to her.

They lay together in the dark, her cheek pressed to his chest and her leg entwined with his. She was in heaven. And she'd like nothing better than to lie in his arms all night. But it was late, and she needed to get back to the hotel before someone came looking for her.

Lu lifted her head and placed a kiss on his stubbled chin. "I'd better go."

"Don't leave. Please. Stay." He cradled her cheek.

"You know why I need to leave." She ran her fingers through his soft, damp hair. "The last thing either of us wants is for the cameras to capture my 'walk of shame' in the morning."

"I'm not ashamed of what we have together, Lu. Are you?"

"No, of course not. I just didn't think you wanted everyone to know your business."

"I don't." He shrugged. "But I do want everyone to know you're mine."

Kace raked her hair to one side so he could get a clear view of her face in the light coming from a bedside lamp. He pressed another kiss to her mouth as he glided his hands up her bare back.

"Does that mean you want…are you asking me—"

"I'm completely enamored with you, Lu. I want to be with you. Just you. And the thought of another man touching you this way drives me insane." His intense gaze met hers. "I don't want to creep around town, pretending we can barely stand each other. I want to take you out for a night on the town. Because that's what you deserve."

He kissed her again, and she could swear she was melting into a puddle of goo.

"Why?" She pulled back from his kiss, her eyes searching his. "Why do you want to be with me, Kace?"

His eyes widened, as if he was shocked that she needed to ask. "Because I see you, Lulu. All of you. You're strong and kind and brave. You're compassionate. You've got an incredibly big heart. There's so much more wit and depth than you show people on TV each week. I wish everyone could see you the way I do."

Tears welled in her eyes, her vision blurring. She couldn't stop the tears that rolled down her cheeks. Her heart felt as if it were swelling inside her chest.

Lulu pressed her mouth to his.

For the first time in a long time, she felt truly seen by a man. Kace could see through all the pretense and bullshit. He appreciated and wanted the woman she was when they were alone, and the hot lights and cameras were turned off. Without the makeup and all of the trappings of the *Secret Lives* lifestyle.

He just wanted *her*. And she wanted him, too.

She had no intention of leaving this bed tonight. Maybe ever.

Ten

Darius had spent the entire morning on one video conference or phone call after another. They'd tweaked the fall line, decided on which garments would be worn together and in which colors. Now they were deciding which of the models engaged for the show should wear each outfit.

The doorbell rang and the delivery person handed him the package he knew contained the prototypes of the swimsuits he'd designed for the show.

He tossed the package on his desk and kept working. He was always a little nervous to see his creations come to life for the first time. There was something amazing about holding a garment in his hand that he'd conceived from beginning to end. If it hit the mark, it was an incredible rush. If it didn't, it was a mentally exhausting letdown. Right now, he couldn't afford either. He needed to stay focused on the job at hand.

Two hours later, he and the team had decided which model would wear each look and the order in which the models would appear. They'd given the swimsuit designs tentative placement in the lineup, until he had the chance to examine each garment and determine if they met the Thr3d standards—both functionally and aesthetically.

Shortly after the conference call, his cell phone rang. He didn't recognize the number.

"Hello?"

"Darius, hi. It's Sophie. I got your number from Kellan. I hope you don't mind."

"No, of course not." He looked up from his laptop where he'd been scrolling through a list of potential music for the runway show. "What can I do for you, Sophie?"

"I don't know how long you plan to be in town, so I wanted to squeeze in some time for us to get to know each other."

"Sure," he said absently. "I'd like that, too."

"I'm going horseback riding at my friend's ranch on the edge of town tomorrow afternoon. Have you ever been horseback riding?"

"No, Sophie," he said patiently with a small chuckle. "It's not a popular activity in Central LA, where I grew up."

"Right." Sophie laughed nervously. "Well, I know you've probably been working like crazy. But I was hoping you could spare a couple of hours to go riding with me."

"I don't know, Soph." The nickname came out without thought. It felt natural. "Tomorrow, I'm simulating a run-through of the entire runway show. I'm not sure I'll be done by early afternoon. My team is a couple of hours behind me in LA."

"When we were volunteering on Saturday, you said yourself that everything is pretty much set for the show. That you're just making yourself crazy by going over every single detail again and again," she reminded him.

He had said that. *Note to self: learn to keep your big mouth shut.*

"C'mon, Darius, it'll be fun. I promise," she continued when he didn't respond. "And it'll give you a chance to explore Royal a bit more. You can't spend your entire stay here locked away in that house. Besides, a little fresh air and brisk activity is good for the creative process. It always spurs new ideas for me or helps me find a solution to whatever design issue I'm trying to tackle."

So this is what it's like to have a little sister.

He could just imagine how Sophie had worked the sad voice and big puppy dog eyes when she was a kid. No wonder Kellan said she had him and Vaughn wrapped around her pinkie finger.

"All right, Sophie. You've convinced me." He leaned back in his chair and glided a hand over his stubbly head. He made a mental note to run a razor over it in the morning. "I'll be there. Just text me the time and location."

"I'll send you a text message shortly."

He could practically hear the victory grin in Sophie's voice when they said their goodbyes.

Darius stood and stretched, walking around the desk. He pressed the heel of his palms to his eyes. Honestly, he could probably use the time away from his computer. He was beginning to go cross-eyed and his brain was in a fog.

Perfect time to shift gears.

Darius opened the package with the four swimsuits. He held each garment up to the light and examined it carefully, testing whether the material was opaque enough. Then he took each individual suit and stretched the material in all four directions.

Everything looks good.

He heard a splash and walked over to the window. It was Audra's first swim since their argument.

He was glad she'd resumed her swimming. Audra had been on her high school and college swim teams and she loved the water. She was practically a mermaid. He hated being the reason she stopped doing something she loved so much.

For her, swimming was moving meditation. She worked her problems out as her hands and feet sliced through the water.

Darius couldn't tear himself from the window. He'd always found watching Audra swim hypnotic and calming. In some small way, she was part of his life again. At least for as long as they were both in Royal.

Darius climbed into his newly rented SUV and drove to Magnolia Acres, as Sophie had directed. Apparently, a longtime friend of his siblings' mother owned the ranch, located on the edge of town.

He'd almost canceled their appointment when Sophie mentioned that Dixie Musgraves—the owner of both the ranch and the home Audra was renting—had been her late mother's best friend. Wouldn't the woman resent him—the product of an affair Buckley Blackwood had behind her best friend's back?

Sophie assured Darius that Dixie didn't blame him for their father's indiscretions. None of them did.

He hadn't been completely convinced, but Sophie was persistent. And there was something about her that made him hate the idea of disappointing her.

So here he was.

Darius parked and climbed out of the black luxury SUV. Unsure what constituted appropriate horse-riding gear, he'd worn his broken-in jeans, a plaid shirt layered over a performance T-shirt and a pair of Thr3d hiking boots. It was a beautiful afternoon; sunny and temperate for March.

He approached the open stables, but no one seemed to be around. "Sophie!" he called.

A couple of the horses looked at him, while the rest seemed unimpressed by his arrival. He couldn't help stopping to stare at them. He'd never been this close to a horse before.

They were beautiful, majestic animals. And much larger than he'd imagined. Even at his height of six-two, the horses' heads towered over his.

After fifteen minutes, he checked his watch. It was ten minutes past the time he and Sophie had agreed to meet.

He'd rearranged his day, started early and gotten nearly everything completed before leaving the house just so he could be here. But if Sophie was just blowing him off, there were tons of things he could be doing instead.

"I'm sorry I'm late, but I was out by the creek on the other end of the ranch doing some sketching and lost track of…" Audra hurried into the stable, breathless, then caught sight of him. "Darius? What are you doing here?"

Strands of her wavy hair clung to her forehead, wet with perspiration. She tucked a few loose strands behind her ear and glanced down at her clothing. Her cheeks turned bright red.

Her light blue shirt was smudged with dirt and there was a smidgen of it on one cheek. Dust and streaks of dirt were on her cropped cargo pants, too. She folded her arms over her chest.

"I'm here to meet my…" His words trailed off quickly and he tugged at the collar of his shirt, allowing cool air inside. "Sophie invited me to go riding. As a way to spark creativity. I've got a problem I've been trying to figure out."

He hated keeping something from Audra again. He kept his words as close to the truth as possible without revealing the nature of his relationship with the Blackwoods.

"That's why she invited me here." Audra narrowed her gaze at him, closing the space between them. "What kind of game are the two of you running?"

Darius folded his arms and studied Audra, who was clearly agitated. "You think I had something to do with this?"

"You keep showing up everywhere I am." She gestured wildly. "How do you explain that?"

"I can't." He shrugged. "But I had no idea you'd be here in Royal. I had no clue you were renting the house next door to the one Miranda provided. I didn't expect to see you at the Texas Cattleman's Club on Saturday, and believe me, I sure as hell didn't expect to see you here." He kept his voice calm.

Audra was a little firecracker who wore her emotions on her sleeve. The most passionate person he'd ever known.

He'd never had a more ardent lover than Audra. She'd ruined him for any woman after her.

"Why should I believe you?" She was asking, her button nose scrunched and her brows furrowed.

"Why would I lie to you about this?"

"Why should you lie to me about *anything*, Darius?" There was hurt in her tone and expression.

"Audra, I'm not lying to you. I really had no idea you'd be here. Trust me, if—"

"How could I possibly trust a man who'd lie about his own parents being dead? Who would do something like that?"

Shit.

His heart thumped in his chest and his pulse raced. "How long have you known?"

"Three years. I read that—"

"Rock magazine article," he finished her statement with a heavy sigh. He wished he could take back that interview. He'd won an award that night, had drunk far too much premium vodka—something he'd stayed away from ever since—and had granted a magazine reporter an impromptu interview.

Darius had said a lot of things he shouldn't have. He'd come off as arrogant and resentful. And he'd talked too honestly about his estranged relationship with his mother and stepfather.

He'd felt awful when he'd read the magazine article. Though he hadn't spoken with his parents much prior to the publication of the article, he'd called to apologize. The upside was that he'd done a better job of staying in contact with them ever since.

He'd call. Briefly inquire after their health. Ask if either of them needed anything. Then he'd tell them that he would get out to see them whenever he could.

Only he never did.

As long as his parents weren't willing to reveal the name of his biological father, he hadn't been able to get over his resentment.

"Audra, I'm sorry. I didn't try to deceive you. I just—"

"You just what, Darius? Explain why'd you'd lie to me about something like that. What kind of sick person—"

"I didn't intend to lie to you, Audra. You asked about my parents, and I told you they were no longer in my life." He shrugged. "A week later I heard you telling a friend my parents were dead. I was going to correct you, but then... I didn't. Because at that time, they were as good as dead to me. I was bitter and angry, and I didn't want anything to do with them." He shrugged. "So rather than creating an embarrassing situation for both of us, I allowed the misunderstanding to stand. It was wrong of me. I realized that rather quickly. But I didn't know how to fix it. If I told you the truth—"

"I'd think you were an ass. Which you are. What could your parents have possibly done to make you so angry with them?"

He opened his mouth to speak, but she cut him off with the wave of her hand.

"Never mind. It doesn't even matter. Anyone who could lie to the person they claimed to love about something like that…" Her voice broke. "I was foolish to believe you ever loved me."

"No, that isn't true." His heart thumped and his pulse raced. He didn't blame Audra for thinking badly of him. He'd been a jerk for the way he'd ended things between them and a liar for allowing her to believe his parents were dead. Still, he couldn't abide her doubting he'd ever really loved her.

"How could you possibly think that I didn't love you?" Darius stepped closer and lightly gripped her shoulders. His eyes searched hers. "You meant everything to me, Audra. Walking away from you was the hardest thing I've ever done."

"Then why'd you do it? If you loved me so much, why'd you walk away?" Her voice trembled and the corners of her eyes were wet with tears.

He dropped his gaze from hers momentarily before forcing his eyes to meet hers again.

"Is it really that hard for you to understand why, Audra?" He dropped his hands from her shoulders. "You're a diamond heiress. The princess of a political dynasty. Your family has more money than God. And I was this poor, scholarship student whose mother tanked her acting career with booze and pills. Not the kind of thing a conservative senator who runs on a family values platform wants for his daughter."

Darius ran a hand over his head, the skin damp with sweat, despite the cool temperature. Revealing the ugly truth that he'd been a coward left him drained.

He'd ended it because he'd known it would only be a matter of time before Audra would move on. She'd eventually find someone who fit into her world and could give her the life she deserved.

He'd wanted to spare them both the pain of getting in any deeper. And he'd thought it would hurt less if he'd ended things on his terms, rather than waiting for the other shoe to fall. That it would lessen the inevitable sting of rejection he knew all too well.

He'd been wrong.

"I never treated you differently, Darius. The money never mattered to me."

"It *did* matter," he countered. "After I insisted on paying for our dates, you didn't want to go to your favorite restaurants anymore. You'd pass on trips with your friends."

"I was being considerate. If you hadn't been so bull-headed, I could've just paid for both of us. I had plenty, and I didn't mind sharing."

"I didn't want you to feel like I was using you."

"Nobody thought that."

"Your friends certainly did."

Her eyes widened, as if she was mortified by his statement, but she didn't deny it. "They told you that?"

"Not in those exact words. But I got the point, just the same." The muscles in his shoulders tensed as he'd recalled the painful memories. "Jessica told me about all of the trips and events you'd skipped because of me. The ones I didn't know about. And your friend Jason wondered aloud how long you planned to 'slum it.'" Darius leaned against one of the empty stalls. "He said it was practically a rich kid rite of passage and that you had a thing for lost causes."

"And you took their word for it? Without even asking me?" she demanded, her voice trembling.

"Not at first. But then I realized that they were right. Eventually, you'd want a man with wealth, power and an upstanding family name. I had none of those, and nothing to give you except for what felt, at the time, like one hell of a long shot. You deserved better than that."

"So is that when you first appointed yourself arbiter of What Audra Deserves?" Her expression was a mixture of sadness, anger and disappointment. "Who your parents are and the number of zeroes in your bank account was never an issue for me, Darius."

"No?" He folded his arms, peering at her intensely.

"How could you even ask me that?"

"Because you never introduced me to your parents when they came to visit you on campus. You never so much as hinted that you wanted me to meet them."

The pain of that long-ago realization still hurt.

"I never... I mean, I didn't..." she stammered.

"You wanted to have this conversation, Audra. So let's have it. You were embarrassed to introduce me to your parents because you knew they'd never approve of you dating me."

"That isn't true. I..." Audra suddenly looked deflated. "I mean...yes, I knew they would think I wasn't being sensible about my future and what was best for the family." She sighed. "I can't even tell you how many times I've heard that line."

"It's okay, babe." He didn't want to hurt her more than he already had. "I understand. Family is a complicated thing. No one knows that more than me. But that's why I walked away. In the end, it was inevitable."

"No, you're wrong." She met his gaze. "I might've been hesitant to tell my parents that I was head over heels for someone they wouldn't have chosen for me. But I *was* going to tell them. I loved you, Darius. I would've done anything for you. I thought you felt the same."

"I did. Audra, I've never loved anyone as much as I loved you."

"But not enough to share your reservations with me. Or enough to tell me the truth about your parents. Not enough to—"

Darius cradled her face and lowered his mouth to hers, silencing her with a kiss. He savored the lips he'd been longing to kiss since he'd set eyes on them in that diner. They were as soft and sweet as he remembered. Flavored by the lip gloss she wore.

Audra tensed in his arms initially, surprised by his sudden action. Though she couldn't have been much more surprised than he was.

He honestly hadn't intended to kiss her. He'd just needed to convince her that what he'd felt for her was real, regardless of what else she might think of him.

Audra tipped her head back, her mouth parting as she wrapped her arms around him.

Darius pressed a hand to her back as his tongue glided against hers and the smooth, round, steel barbell that pierced it. A jolt of desire ran through his body at the sensation. She clutched at the back of his shirt, erasing the sliver of space between their bodies. And he soon lost himself in the warmth of her embrace, the hunger in her kiss.

He'd missed everything about this woman.

The feel of her. The taste of her. The way she'd made him feel.

Darius was relieved by her reaction. If she'd given the slightest indication the kiss was unwanted, he would've apologized for reading her wrong and never laid a hand on her again. But instead of withdrawing, Audra curled deeper into him. She welcomed his kiss with a sweet little murmur, as if she couldn't get enough. The vibration of that carnal sound sent a shiver down his spine, his body responding to hers.

He teetered backward, his back pressed against the post behind him. She moved closer, eliminating the space created by the shift in his position.

Darius glided a hand beneath her shirt. His fingertips caressed the soft, smooth skin on her back. His other hand inched downward, resting just short of the curvy ass that left him mesmerized every time she walked away from him. Her figure was a little fuller now than it had been five years ago. But the additional weight suited her, having settled in all the right places.

He kissed her harder. Deeper. Both of them were breathing heavily, but too consumed with the passion rising between them to stop.

Audra's hands glided up his chest and she fumbled with the buttons on his shirt. She slipped one button through its snug hole. Then another. And another.

His mind raced, and his heart thumped wildly. The sound of his own heartbeat filled his ears.

He wanted her. *Desperately.*

Darius ached to examine every inch of her fuller frame. To feel her body beneath his. To relive the indescribable pleasure of being inside her. But he'd imagined it too long to settle for a quick roll in the literal hay with Mr. Ed and his friends watching.

"Audra, I—" He stopped suddenly.

Was that the sound of tires on gravel?

"What is it?" Audra frowned, her breathing ragged.

"I think someone is coming." He loosened his grip on her.

"Oh." She stepped beyond his reach, smoothing her hair back and rubbing at the stray gloss around her lips.

Lip gloss. Shit.

He rubbed at his mouth with the back of his hand as Sophie and Nigel strode into the stables hand in hand.

"There you two are. I thought you might've started down the trail without us, since neither of you responded to my text message that we were running late." Sophie's gaze went from Darius to Audra and back again.

He'd left his phone in the truck, not wanting it to get jostled as he rode a horse. And he hadn't felt Audra's phone in any of her pockets as she'd pressed against him.

"Nigel had to handle some last-minute business with the show," Sophie continued, when neither of them spoke. "I hope we haven't inconvenienced either of you too much."

"Actually…" Audra said, "I'm beat. I've been out here most of the day. I just want to take a long bath. Maybe turn in early tonight."

"Of course. I'm sorry we kept you waiting." Sophie's brows furrowed and she glanced between them again, as if trying to determine if something had gone wrong. "Rain check?"

"Absolutely." Audra smiled at Sophie. The two women hugged. "Goodbye, Nigel." She nodded at the man, but then barely cast a glance in Darius's direction as she called out, "Goodbye, Darius."

Audra was gone before he could blink.

"Sorry we interrupted," Sophie said, breaking into his thoughts.

"Interrupted?" It was best to plead ignorance.

Sophie exchanged a knowing look with her fiancé, then gestured to her face. "You have her lip gloss all over your mouth."

Darius scrubbed at his mouth and the area surrounding it with the back of his hand again. This time harder.

He was glad Sophie didn't ask what had happened between him and Audra. Though his lip gloss–stained lips told the story well enough.

"Now it's time for your first riding lesson." His sister grinned. "I'll show you how to strap on a saddle."

Darius followed Sophie to one of the stalls, which housed a majestic horse with a shiny black coat. He listened as Sophie schooled him on the horse he'd be riding and gave him pointers on warming up to the animal.

But he was only thinking of Audra and the bitter words she'd flung at him prior to their kiss.

If you loved me so much, why'd you walk away?

I loved you, Darius. I would've done anything for you. I thought you felt the same.

The heat and passion between them were as intense as ever. But he'd wounded Audra, and she no longer trusted him. He'd wrecked their relationship, and there was no one but himself to blame.

Eleven

Audra paced just inside the front door of her rental home. She'd kissed Darius in the stables three days ago, and she hadn't seen him since. In fact, she'd gone out of her way to avoid him. That included not swimming for the past three days.

Now she was restless. Partly because her routine had been disrupted. Partly because her daily swims helped her to blow off steam. And partly because she hadn't been able to stop thinking of that kiss.

Darius was such an amazing kisser.

There was something in his kiss that was hungry, yet tender. She never understood how he managed that. She only knew that she'd never had a kiss quite like it. And though her head knew that the last thing she needed was to kiss Darius again, her heart and her body craved it.

Audra dragged a hand through her hair and sighed.

She was being ridiculous. There was no need for her to avoid Darius. They were two reasonable adults whose relationship didn't work out.

Shit happened.

But they could still be cordial. They could see each other around town and maybe even laugh off the kiss.

Audra checked the clock. Sophie was expecting her at the TCC clubhouse in half an hour for more restoration work. She didn't know whether Darius intended to be there, but she wouldn't tiptoe around on eggshells trying to avoid him anymore. So they might as well get the awkward conversation over.

She made her way to his place. Eyes closed briefly, she sucked in a deep breath and rang the bell.

Audra knew he was there, but part of her hoped he wouldn't answer the door. She heard movement inside.

No such luck.

She could see him through the glass pane. He paused momentarily, his eyes widening.

"Audra, hey." He leaned against the doorframe. "What can I do for you?"

"Can we talk?"

"Sure." He gestured for her to come inside. "I'm heading out in a few minutes."

"Going to the TCC clubhouse for volunteer duty? Me, too," she said when he'd nodded in response. "That's why I thought we should talk. If we get paired together again, I don't want things to be weird between us."

He rubbed the sexy scruff on his chin, and she instantly recalled the scrape of his stubbly beard against her skin when they'd kissed.

"I'm glad you came by, Audra. I wanted to apologize. I shouldn't have kissed you. I made an awkward situation unbearable."

"I appreciate the apology, but it isn't necessary. After all, I kissed you back." She shrugged as if it were no big deal, refusing to acknowledge the racing of her pulse. "We got caught up in the moment."

"Yeah, I guess we did."

Heat flared in her chest and her belly tensed as they stared at each other, neither of them speaking. Finally, Darius broke the silence.

"Still, I shouldn't have...and it won't happen again. So there's no need for you to stop using the pool. I screwed things up between us, but I honestly do care for you." He sighed. "I hope that we can be friends."

"I'd like that." She nodded.

Darius checked his watch, then grabbed his keys off the kitchen counter. "It's getting late. We'd better head out."

She couldn't help smiling. Darius hated being late. In fact, he was usually early for everything.

"You know, it's silly for both of us to drive when we're headed to the same place. Why don't I give you a ride to the clubhouse?" Audra tried not to sound eager.

"Or I could give you one. Your driving still makes me a little nervous." He chuckled.

Audra laughed, the tension between them easing slightly. "It isn't my driving that makes you nervous. It's the fact that you aren't in control. Same reason you don't love flying."

"Maybe there's some truth to that." Darius massaged the back of his neck. "But I had to get over it. The flying thing I mean. I had to hop a plane with a moment's notice to meet with investors in the beginning. So I finally read that book you gave me on nervous flyers. It helped. I hardly think about it anymore."

"I'm glad. And I accept your offer. Let me close up the house, then I'll meet you at your SUV."

Darius agreed, his mouth cocked in a wry grin that did things to her.

It's just a ride into town.

They'd be alone in the car together five minutes each way. Ten, tops. She could certainly keep her head, and legs, together that long.

Still, Darius Taylor-Pratt was her personal Kryptonite. She needed to maintain emotional distance from the man. Or else she was going to need to get herself a damned good lead suit.

"Audra, you look rather happy this morning." Sophie grinned as she dispensed coffee into two mugs.

"Good morning, Sophie."

Audra liked Sophie Blackwood. She could imagine them becoming friends. So she didn't want to hurt Sophie's feelings, but they needed to have a serious conversation.

"Could we talk for a sec?" Audra stepped closer and lowered her voice.

"Uh-oh." Sophie put the mugs back on the table. "You're upset about the other day."

"I'm not upset." Audra touched the woman's arm. "I realize that you're happy and in love and you think everyone else should be, too. But Darius and I had our chance. It didn't work out for us. We're both okay with that."

"Are you?" Sophie asked. "I mean, I know it's none of my business, but we couldn't help noticing that your lip gloss was smudged on Darius's face. You two were obviously kissing before we arrived."

Audra's face heated. She cleared her throat. "Darius and I talked this morning. It was a mistake neither of us plans to repeat. I appreciate your concern, but we're both good with things the way they are."

"I hope I haven't caused any problems between you." Sophie sounded incredibly sad.

"Everything is fine. In fact, we rode in together this morning. Just because it made sense," she added.

"All right," Sophie agreed begrudgingly. "No more shenanigans from me. Scout's honor." She touched three fingers to her forehead in a Scout salute.

"Thanks, Sophie. Now tell me where you need me this morning."

"Come with me. I've got just the spot for you."

A slow smile spread across Sophie's face and her brown eyes danced mischievously. Audra groaned quietly. Despite the other woman's promise, something told Audra that her plea to Sophie had fallen on deaf ears.

"Thanks for volunteering again today." Kellan approached as Darius filled his mug with steaming hot coffee.

"No problem. How's your wife?" Darius inquired.

"Mornings are tough for Irina right now. But she's anxious to meet you. She wants me to invite you for dinner one evening."

"Sounds great. Let's shoot for a date after Fashion Week. Right now, even when I'm not working, my brain is running through everything and trying to head off a million ways the show could go wrong."

"Sounds like a lot of pressure." Kellan sipped his coffee.

"It is." Darius added two packets of sugar to his cup. "But I enjoy the entire process. It's just the nature of the business. I'm fortunate to be doing work I love."

"Can't ask for much more than that in life." Kellan set his empty coffee mug with the other dirty ones. "There's one other thing that Sophie and I would like to talk to you about."

"Oh?" Darius sipped his hot coffee. His gut tensed at Kellan's serious tone. "What is it?"

"It's about our father's estate. As you know, the old bastard cut us out of the will and left everything to his ex-wife." Kellan tried to maintain an even temperament, but even without knowing the man well, Darius could tell that he was seething beneath that cool facade.

"Yes. What of it?" Darius hadn't talked about money or the estate with either Sophie or Kellan. He didn't want them thinking he was only after a payday.

"Miranda was married to our father for a short time. The house, the land it sits on, the Blackwood Bank... none of those things should go to her. They should stay in the family." Kellan frowned deeply, and his blue eyes turned stormy. The crinkles around his narrowed gaze, filled with pain, made him look considerably older than he had moments ago. "Sophie, Vaughn and I put up with a lot of shit from our dad over the years. So did our mother. Those holdings are part of our family's legacy. That's why Sophie and I are contesting the will. And we'd like you to join us in the claim against Miranda."

"I see." Darius sipped his coffee. His mind spun as he considered what Kellan was asking of him.

Miranda had made it clear that she had a genuine interest in partnering with his company. If he joined his siblings in contesting the will, he could kiss the deal with Miranda's Goddess brand goodbye.

There was a hell of a lot of money at stake.

According to his personal lawyer, Blackwood's estate was worth hundreds of millions of dollars, even split between the four siblings.

But the deal with Miranda would also be extremely lucrative—not just for him personally, but for his employees and the investors who'd believed in his vision from the start. And creating a line for the Goddess brand could be the springboard that would prompt other companies to collaborate with Thr3d to create their clothing lines, too.

"What's Vaughn's position on this?" Darius asked.

Kellan laughed bitterly. "He wants nothing to do with our father's legacy. If Vaughn up and changed the name of his company from Blackwood Energy to something else completely, I'd hardly be surprised. His position is that Miranda should enjoy whatever portion of the inheritance would've gone to him. Sophie and I, clearly, don't agree."

Darius hated to disappoint his new brother. He liked Kellan and Sophie and relished the kinship he felt with them. But he had an obligation to his business. He'd spent most of his adult life constructing what he hoped would one day be a billion-dollar international brand.

He couldn't allow the warm, fuzzy feelings toward his newfound family to destroy everything he'd built. Not now, when it felt like his goal was in reach.

"Look, Kellan, I appreciate that you and Sophie want me to join in on the claim. That's generous of you, given the circumstances. But the reason I came here was to partner with Miranda and her Goddess brand. If I join you and Sophie in the suit against her—"

"You'll blow the deal." Kellan groaned quietly and shrugged one shoulder. "I get it. You've known us all of two weeks. You've probably been working toward a deal like this for years."

"Exactly. And I'm not saying that I won't do it. Just that I need some time to weigh out the pros and cons. My entire team is depending on me. I can't make a decision on a whim just because I'm incredibly fond of both of you. I hope you understand."

"I do." Kellan nodded. "We'll respect your choice, either way. It doesn't change the fact that you're our brother, and we want you to be part of our lives."

"Thanks." Darius's shoulders relaxed. He really did like both Kellan and Sophie. "Can I get back to you on this in a few weeks?"

"Fine by me. I think Sophie would be okay with it, too." Kellan glanced toward where Sophie was waving the two of them over. "It appears we're being summoned." Kellan nodded toward their sister.

Darius finished his coffee and discarded his cup. As he approached Sophie, there was a mischievous glint in her eyes.

Please, no more of Sophie's unsolicited matchmeddling.

"Good morning, Kellan and Darius. We have new work assignments." Sophie consulted the clipboard in her hand.

"Okay," Darius said cautiously, his belly tensing with the suspicion that his sister was up to something. "Just tell me where you need me."

"We'll be working in the gardens again, but with different partners this time."

"Who am I working with this morning?"

Sophie's grin deepened. "Rafaela Marchesi." She swept her hand in the direction of a beautiful woman, who he'd guess was about ten years his senior. She stood about three inches shy of his height and had cascading waves of thick brown hair.

The woman grinned and her eyes, the color of root beer, danced as she surveyed him. She extended a hand for him to kiss.

He held it in both of his instead. "It's a pleasure to meet you Ms. Marchesi. I look forward to working with you."

"Likewise, Darius." The woman smiled, seemingly amused that he'd politely dodged kissing her hand.

She was statuesque, with her hourglass figure and perfect posture. Her designer skinny jeans clung to her frame and her off-shoulder blouse nicely complemented her shape.

Rafaela slipped her arm through his. "And please, I must insist that you call me Rafaela."

"I will." He nodded. Something about the hungry way in which the woman scanned his frame made him feel naked.

"Audra, there you are." Sophie called to her as she entered the outdoor space.

His gaze met Audra's and then hers zeroed in on the woman's arm wrapped around his. The easy smile on her face turned to a scowl momentarily. But then she forced a smile.

"You haven't lost your partner already, have you?" Sophie teased.

Tripp, the man who'd been so fascinated with Audra

the previous week, suddenly appeared. He handed her a bottle of water.

Darius's hands curled into fists at his sides suddenly and his jaw clenched. He shifted his gaze to Sophie, who was smiling like a Cheshire cat.

Well played, Sophie.

"Darius, you must tell me all about your company. Sophie tells me that you're a designer and that you'll be doing a show at LA Fashion Week. How fabulous," Rafaela was saying as she led him to the far side of the garden. "Of course, you must know that before I joined the cast of *Secret Lives*, I was a model myself."

Rafaela is a member of the Secret Lives *cast?*

"No, I wasn't aware." He really needed to catch an episode or two of the show, if for no other reason than to be able to identify any other cast members he might run into around town. "But it doesn't surprise me."

Her smile widened, as her grip on his bicep tightened. "You're a very handsome man, Darius. Have you ever been married?"

He sucked in a deep breath and sighed.

It's going to be an incredibly long day.

Twelve

Audra worked with Tripp to replant new bushes. Her new partner was handsome, to say the least. But he was also well aware of it. Yet, despite his cocky, flirtatious, uninhibited nature, Tripp was funny. They'd spent a good portion of the afternoon laughing.

The two of them had been teamed up with his sister, Tessa, and her husband, Ryan Bateman. They were an adorable couple. Down-to-earth, sweet and funny. The three of them had kept Audra in stitches with their antics. When she learned Ryan had lived next door to Tripp and Tessa's family and the three of them had been friends practically since infancy, she wasn't surprised. Their love and friendship was evident, especially in their teasing banter.

It only made sense that Ryan and Tessa had eventually fallen for each other. She envied their love. It was apparent that their relationship had been built on friendship first.

Audra was not quite thirty, but in recent years, more and more of her friends and cousins were getting married. She'd started to think more about settling down and raising a family of her own.

She glanced over at Darius, who was working with former model Rafaela Marchesi. The woman touched Darius every chance she got, and she drank in his physique like it was a thousand-dollar bottle of champagne and someone else was paying the tab.

Of course, Rafaela had five ex-husbands and was a star on the *Secret Lives of NYC Ex-Wives* reality show filming in town. So someone else undoubtedly *was* paying the tab. The way she looked at Darius, Rafaela was evidently cruising for her sixth husband and considered Darius a good prospect.

"Audra." Tripp touched her shoulder and she nearly jumped out of her skin. "Sorry, I didn't mean to startle you, but I called you several times and you didn't hear me. They're about to serve lunch."

"Sorry. I was lost in thought." Her cheeks heated under the knowing grins of Tessa and Ryan. Tripp seemed far less amused. "You don't need to wait for me. I'm just going to finish planting this last bush, then I'll be right in."

"We'll catch up to you guys," Tripp told his sister and his brother-in-law as everyone else in the yard, including Darius and Rafaela headed inside. "Save us a place."

Ryan nodded, then slipped his arm around Tessa and headed toward the building.

Tripp helped her set the last bush into the ground and then filled the hole with dirt. Then she watered it.

"Thanks for waiting for me, Tripp." Audra removed her gloves and slid her sunglasses on top of her head. "But you didn't need to. You're probably starving."

"After all of the work we did this morning, I'll bet you are, too." He removed his own gloves and put them with their tools. They both headed inside. "So, that Darius guy...how long ago did you two break up?"

She tensed a little. It was no secret that she and Darius had been a couple. Sophie had told Tripp and the others as much when they'd volunteered last week. Still, it felt odd to talk to Tripp about it. Especially when she was having a myriad of conflicting feelings about Darius.

"Five years," she said finally. "Sometimes it feels like it was a lifetime ago. Other times—"

"It feels like it was just yesterday?" His light brown eyes twinkled in the sun. "I've been there before. Must've been weird for you, running into him here after all this time."

"It was. It is," she stammered. "But I think we've come to an understanding."

"Is that why you've been staring at Rafaela all morning like you're ready to drag her all over the yard by her extensions?"

"I was *not* looking at her that way," Audra protested. When he stared at her incredulously, she sighed. "Okay, so maybe I was. It wasn't intentional."

Or maybe I don't have things worked out as well as I thought.

"I know you didn't ask for my advice, and if you don't want it, feel free to tell me to shut the hell up." He stopped, just before they stepped inside the building.

Audra studied Tripp's face. She barely knew him.

Why should she care that he'd noticed her staring flaming daggers at Rafaela Marchesi? And who cared about his advice on the subject?

Evidently, she did.

"Okay, Wise One." She folded her arms and tipped her chin. "What say you?"

A wide grin spread across his handsome face. "Be honest with the guy and with yourself. Whatever it is you're feeling, just…feel it. Don't pretend the feelings aren't there. Wade through them, rather than trying to find a way around them. That'll only get you stuck in the quicksand. If you don't tackle your emotions head-on, they'll sabotage future relationships."

"Wow. That was remarkably insightful." She narrowed her gaze at him. "I wasn't expecting that."

"I am so misunderstood and underappreciated, I might add." He laughed, the sound filling the courtyard. "I happen to be a font of fantastic relationship advice. I just haven't worked out the whole applying-it-to-myself thing, yet."

"Yeah, I get that." Audra couldn't help laughing, too. "I guess I'm surprised because…" She shrugged, her words trailing off. "I don't know."

"Because I'm obviously attracted to you. So you didn't expect me to do something as selfless as suggest you be honest about your feelings for your old flame?" Tripp folded his arms.

"Something like that."

"Then let me set your mind at ease. I'm not being selfless. I'd love to spend time one-on-one with you, Audra. But if we ever do, I don't want that guy lingering in your head," he said with a self-assured smirk.

"You know, Tripp Noble, you're much deeper than

you let on." Audra smiled. "And thank you for the excellent advice."

"That must net me a hug or something." He opened his arms wide.

Audra laughed and hugged Tripp before they headed inside to wash their hands and join the others for lunch.

Tripp was right. Her declaration earlier that everything was fine between her and Darius was complete and utter bullshit. She had a ton of feelings for Darius that she still hadn't worked out. Things she still wanted to say to him.

Maybe the reason she'd been unable to make a deeper connection with Cash was because she still hadn't worked out her feelings about Darius.

She'd been lodged in quicksand for the past five years, just as Tripp had indicated.

Audra wasn't sure how or when, but now that she knew what needed to be done, she had every intention of working out the doubts and lingering emotions that had plagued her since her and Darius's sudden breakup.

Whatever the results of their conversation, at least she'd finally be able to move on.

At the end of the day, Audra, Tripp, Tessa and Ryan cleaned up their space and returned the tools they'd been using. Audra had put away a small load of tools when Darius approached.

"Hey, Audra, I wondered if you still planned to ride home with me?" he asked tentatively.

"Of course. Why wouldn't I? Or do you have plans with Rafaela now?" Her gut suddenly twisted at the thought. "If so, I'm sure I can find a ride with someone else."

"No, I don't have plans with Rafaela." He lowered his head and whispered conspiratorially, "And don't say her name too many times, or I have a sneaking suspicion she'll suddenly appear."

"Who is she, Beetlejuice?" She couldn't help giggling.

"Don't know, and I don't want to find out." He chuckled.

"All I'm saying is, you don't have to try so hard to get rid of me." Audra forced a smile. "If your plans have changed, I understand."

"I asked because I thought maybe *your* plans had changed." He rubbed the back of his neck.

"Why?" She fell in line beside him as he walked back toward the clubhouse.

He hesitated before responding. "I wasn't spying on you or anything, but I saw you hug Tripp."

It was petty, but she felt a slight sense of satisfaction that Darius felt a twinge of jealousy, too. "I was thanking him. He helped me out with something."

"Oh. Well, I just need to talk to a couple of people before we leave." He checked his watch. "Meet you at the door in ten?"

She nodded as she watched him walk away, spending a little more time admiring his ass than she should have.

"Seems that absence does indeed make the heart grow fonder." Sophie approached out of nowhere, startling Audra.

"Sophie!" Audra dragged a hand over her head. "You scared me to death."

"Guess you didn't hear me calling you because you were too busy studying Darius's derriere." Sophie grinned mischievously. "The man you supposedly have zero interest in."

"Doesn't mean my eyes don't work." Audra glanced longingly in Darius's direction one more moment before turning to face Sophie's incredulous stare. "Fine, maybe I do still have feelings for him. That doesn't mean we're right for each other."

"Relationships are scary, I get it." Sophie's expression softened. "But there's only one way to find out if there's something there. And avoiding each other isn't it."

"I know," Audra said quietly. She turned to face Sophie head-on. "And I'm going to talk to Darius, but I don't need your push or pull to do it."

"Yes, ma'am." Sophie smiled. "Think I need to apologize to Darius for putting Rafaela Marchesi on his trail?"

They both laughed.

"No, he'll be fine. We both will. No matter what happens."

"I know. I guess I just want everyone to be as happy and in love as Nigel and I are." Sophie beamed. "By the way, the final design for our rings is so beautiful. It was the perfect compromise. I can't thank you enough for coming here and designing them."

"My pleasure." Audra squeezed Sophie's hand. "My team has been working hard on your custom pieces. In a few days, I'll return to Dallas to pick up your rings. Hopefully, all of your bridal party jewelry will be completed by then. Once you've approved all of the pieces, I'll head back to Dallas."

"That's wonderful!" Sophie clapped her hands excitedly, but then her expression suddenly changed. "Wait, you aren't staying for the wedding?"

"I don't typically attend my client's weddings, Sophie. This entire experience is far different than anything I've done before."

"Then why not make another exception? Stay for the wedding." Sophie's eyes pleaded. "Besides, I don't just think of you as my jewelry designer. Since you've been here, you've become a friend."

Audra was touched by the woman's words. "I feel the same."

"Then stay, please. You've already leased Dixie's place for the rest of the month. Might as well enjoy it."

"It is a beautiful town, and everyone here is so nice," Audra had to admit. "A girl could become accustomed to this."

Sophie's eyes danced. "Then why don't you make Royal your new home?"

"What?" Audra laughed. "I said I liked it here, Sophie. I didn't say I was ready to relocate."

"Why not?" Sophie asked matter-of-factly. "We're a stone's throw from Dallas, so it would be easy enough to access your shop. Besides, you already said you like it here more than Dallas. And everyone around here really likes you."

"And being here has been great. But moving here? I don't know about that."

"Well, it's not like you have to decide today," the younger woman said. "But if you did, there would be a whole lot of us ready to welcome you."

"It means the world to me that you want me here. And if I ever do decide to pull up stakes, I promise to give Royal serious consideration."

"That's all I ask." Sophie seemed pleased with her answer. She nodded toward the door. "Your chariot awaits."

Darius looked handsome, if a little tired, as he stood by the front door, patiently waiting for her.

They chatted cordially about their day during the short ride home. It was over before she could blink.

She was dirty and tired, and she needed a bath and a nap. But when Darius turned off the engine, she honestly wasn't ready to end their time together. She'd forgotten how much she enjoyed just being with him. There'd always been something so calming about his presence. It balanced out her high-intensity personality.

"How are the runway show plans coming?" she asked, needing a reason to spend just a few minutes more in his company.

"Everything is going according to plan so far, despite four last-minute additions that I'm hoping will be showstoppers."

"That's a bold move," she said. "What did you add to the show, if you don't mind me asking?"

"I don't." His gaze lingered on hers for a moment and it warmed something deep inside her chest. "But I'd rather show you. Come in for an early nightcap?"

"I'd love to, but I'm filthy and tired." She forced a laugh, fighting back the sadness she felt at turning down his offer. Talking to Darius about his upcoming show over a glass of wine sounded like a lovely way to spend the evening. And a great opportunity to finish the conversation they'd begun in the stables. This time, hopefully, there would be no tongue involved.

"I'm heading straight for the shower, too. But I'd love to show you what you inspired me to add to the show."

"Me?"

"Yes, you, Audra." He chuckled. "Don't act so surprised. I'm sure I'm not the first man you've inspired, and I won't likely be the last."

"I'm intrigued," she said finally. "If I don't pass out from sheer exhaustion after my shower, I'll drop by."

"Perfect." The glint of victory was in his dark eyes. He knew her well enough to know her curiosity would get the better of her. "I have a few bottles chilling in the wine fridge, and I'll leave the patio door unlocked."

They parted ways, and Audra headed straight for the laundry. She peeled off the layers of filthy clothing and dropped them into the washing machine. Then she got into the steaming hot shower. Audra hummed softly, as the hot water cascaded over her. Her skin tingled with excitement in anticipation of spending more time with Darius.

Thirteen

Audra slipped on a simple denim shift minidress. It was adorable but also sexy without looking as if she was trying too hard.

She pulled her still-damp, wavy hair into a high ponytail, slipped on a pair of sandals with a low heel and applied her lip gloss.

Audra opened the iron gate that separated their backyards. It was strange to make her way directly toward the house, since she usually made a point of not glancing in that direction on her way to the pool.

The lights were on in the family room and in the space she knew to be the office. Despite her efforts not to, she'd sometimes caught a glimpse of him working there.

Audra inhaled deeply, then knocked on the patio door's metal frame.

No answer.

She slid the door open and stepped inside.

"Darius?"

She called him twice more. Still, no answer.

Audra ventured in the direction of his office. The door was open, and the light was on, so she stepped inside.

The space was neat and organized. His laptop was on the desk, closed. Two dry-erase boards and a large corkboard dominated the walls. She approached the corkboard where four swimsuits were pinned. Audra didn't touch them, fearful the entire board would fall. She shifted her attention to the sketches posted. Two male figures and two female figures wore the designs pinned on the board. She studied the female figures.

There wasn't a ton of detail. Just enough that the woman felt familiar.

"Audra." Darius stood beside her. "I didn't hear you come in."

"I knocked, and I called you when I stepped inside, but you didn't respond." She turned to face him. "I hope it's okay that I let myself in."

"Of course. I got a late start on that shower. My assistant called with a few questions."

"This late in the day on a Saturday?"

"It's not as late there, but yeah, she's about as obsessive as I am." He chuckled. "It's why we work so well together. Besides, I give each employee a stake in the company. I find it makes them more invested in the outcomes."

"So Thr3d is a privately owned company?"

"It is. And I'll keep it that way for as long as it makes

sense." He stepped farther inside the room. The scent of his shower gel tickled her nostrils.

Audra turned back toward the board with the sketches. "That's me, isn't it?"

"Sometimes, when my brain felt all tied in knots, I'd watch you swim," he admitted, not responding to her question directly. "There's something soothing about how gracefully your arms and legs cut through the water. And then one day I got the idea to create a few swimwear pieces for the lineup."

"I didn't think Thr3d carried swimwear."

"We haven't. At least, not until now. And maybe we never will." He shrugged. "Depends on how they're received."

"You started these designs from scratch since you arrived?" She looked back at him.

"I did. It was a risky move, but your passion for swimming…it motivated me. I couldn't let the idea alone until I saw it through."

"Your team must've really loved that," Audra teased.

He grinned. "I've undoubtedly been called some very unsavory names behind my back these past couple of weeks. But now everyone is pleased with the way things turned out."

"May I?" She indicated the one-piece swimming suit.

"Please." He unpinned the garment and handed it to Audra. "Since you were the inspiration for the piece, I'd love to get your honest, unfiltered opinion."

"Have you ever known me to offer any other kind?"

"No." Darius chuckled, rubbing his chin.

The sensation of his scruff sensitizing her flesh in the barn that day ghosted over her skin, and she shivered.

"Your candidness is one of the things I appreciate most about you," he said.

"Then why didn't you give me the same courtesy? Didn't you think I deserved that much?" The words escaped her mouth before she could reel them back in.

Audra wanted to finish their conversation. She really did. But she'd hoped to at least get a glass of wine out of the deal first. Perhaps that would've taken the edge off of her tone. It was an honest question. She wasn't looking for confrontation.

Darius sat on the edge of a black filing cabinet, suddenly seeming to need more space between them. His eyes were filled with regret and perhaps shame.

"It's like I told you at the stables. The lie about my parents—it began as a misunderstanding and then…it sort of became my shield." He shrugged. "Suddenly, my ugly, messy history had been erased, and I didn't need to talk about it. I was happier with you than I'd been in a long time. I didn't want to ruin it."

"And if we'd stayed together…would you have just gone on lying to me?"

"No, of course not. But I was afraid that once you knew the truth, it'd be over between us."

"I would've been hurt, naturally. But if you'd just been honest with me…" Audra shook her head, the words dying on her lips.

What good will it do either of us to rehash the past?

She stood in front of Darius. "I didn't come here to argue. But for the past five years, I've been pretending I'm fine. Telling myself it was all just water under the bridge. But that isn't true. I loved you, Darius. When you suddenly declared that we were over, with no real explanation, it felt as if our relationship never mattered to you. Like *I* never mattered to you. That's what I've struggled to get past. How could I have been so wrong?"

Unshed tears stung her eyes and clouded her vision. She turned away from him, but he grasped her wrist.

"You weren't wrong, Audra." His voice was a rough whisper as he tugged her toward him, forcing her to meet his gaze. He placed her hand over his heart. "I loved you so much. But I'd had so much rejection in my life. I couldn't bear the thought of being rejected by the person I loved most."

Audra swallowed hard and wet her lips. Her chest heaved with shallow breaths. "I understand now why you believed I would've done that. I'd always given in to my parents' wishes. But I'd decided that I wasn't going to give you up. I was going to tell them about us, I swear. I just needed time."

"I believe you, sweetheart." His eyes didn't leave hers. "I screwed up. I should've told you how I—"

Audra pressed her lips to his. She didn't want contrition, she wanted *this*. His mouth on hers as her trembling hands cradled his face.

Darius slipped his arms around her waist, pulling her closer, so that she stood between his legs. He pressed his large hands to her back as he kissed her. His strong hands glided down and cupped her bottom, pulling her flush against him. Erasing the space between them.

Audra tugged the hem of his shirt up, pressing her fingers to his bare back. She glided her hands over the muscles beneath his skin. Relished the terrain that was familiar, and yet much different than before.

Darius broke their kiss, just long enough to help her tug his shirt over his head and toss it onto the floor.

"Someone has been working out." She squeezed his biceps before kissing him again.

"Had to do something with all of that frustration," he muttered, between kisses to her neck and shoulder.

"Funny, I did just the opposite. I ate my feelings. Thus the additional pounds." She'd gained nearly ten pounds in that first year. They'd been joined by another ten over the course of the next four years, though the swimming kept the weight gain gradual.

"I liked your body just fine before. But I'm mesmerized by it now." He kissed his way down her chest, unbuttoning the three buttons on the placard of the dress and giving himself better access.

He kissed the top of one breast as he tugged the collar of the dress to one side, exposing more of her shoulder.

Audra's heart was racing. There was a dull, steady pulse between her thighs. Like a heartbeat. Her beaded nipples tingled with anticipation.

As much as she already missed his lips on hers, she eagerly anticipated the sensation of him taking one of her painfully hard nipples into his mouth. Thoughts of all the other ways he could use that amazing mouth made her head spin.

She pulled just out of his grip. For a moment, he seemed panicked, as if he was worried he'd upset her. Or maybe he thought she'd changed her mind. But instead, she gripped the bottom of the dress and pulled it up over her hips.

Darius put his hands over hers, halting her progress. His breathing was ragged.

"Audra, are you sure this is what you want?" His warm breath tickled her skin as his lips grazed her ear.

It was good they hadn't had any wine yet. Neither of them would have reason to doubt her decision.

Audra nodded. "Yes. Take me to bed, Darius. Now. Please."

For an instant, she regretted adding the little plea at the end. She wouldn't grovel before the man who'd lied to and rejected her. But as she stared into his eyes, it was clear she was the one who had complete control.

Audra had always loved the way Darius looked at her. Especially when they'd made love. He'd regarded her as if there wasn't anything in the world that he wanted more. She felt that now: desired, appreciated. A reflection of just how intensely she wanted him, too.

He helped her yank the fabric over her head and toss it onto the floor. Darius studied her, as she stood there in a black lace bra and cheeky little black lace boy shorts that provided plenty of coverage from the front but left very little to the imagination from the back.

From the tenting of the front panel of his athletic shorts, he obviously enjoyed the view.

He stood and opened his hand, extending it to her.

Audra placed her hand in his, willing the trembling in her limbs and the butterflies in her belly to stop.

Darius took her to the master bedroom on the other side of the house and laid her on the bed. He stripped off his shorts, revealing a pair of stretch boxers with Dolce & Gabbana printed on the waistband.

He crawled onto the bed, hovering over her. He pressed one kiss to her lips and then another. And another.

Sliding the band from her ponytail, he sifted his fingers through her hair as he kissed her, his tongue seeking hers and licking at the barbell piercing. His thick, hard erection pressed against her thigh.

She wanted him. More than she wanted anything else in that moment. She wouldn't let herself think beyond that. Otherwise, she'd begin to question herself. To question him. But right now, she didn't want to think. She only wanted to feel.

Darius flipped onto his back, pulling her on top of him without breaking their kiss. His hands glided up and down her back. He gripped her bottom, pulling her against his hardened shaft.

She sucked in a deep breath at the delicious sensation of his steely length pressed against her heated, sensitive flesh—the feeling so much more intense now than before. There was a fluttering low in her belly and electricity zipped along her spine.

Audra whimpered, the sound lost in their increasingly fervent kiss.

"You have no idea how badly I want you." He pushed aside the curtain of dark brown hair that blocked his view of her face. "I haven't been able to stop thinking about you since—"

"The diner?" She hadn't been able to stop thinking of him since then, either.

"No matter how hard I try to push you out of my head…you're always there."

Audra felt that way, too. Since long before they'd crossed paths at that diner.

She'd smiled and gone on with her life for the past five years. Started her dream business. Found success. Tried to find love again. But inside, she'd been splintered and falling apart, trying to hide the devastation.

Whatever it is you're feeling, just...feel it. Don't pretend the feelings aren't there.

Audra pressed her mouth to his again and kissed him. She was done talking.

Darius unfastened her bra and slipped it from her shoulders. Then he rolled her onto her back and trailed kisses down her chest. He took one beaded tip into his warm mouth, sucking it, then teasing it with his tongue as she squirmed beneath him.

He slowly kissed his way down her belly, flicking the dangling, diamond butterfly belly ring with his tongue. The pulsing between her thighs beat like a drum.

Darius tugged the lacy material down her thighs and tossed it onto the floor. When he spread her with his thumbs and tasted her there, she gasped at the intense pleasure. Audra dug her heels into the mattress, her hips straining toward his mouth.

A silent plea for more.

Legs trembling and heart racing, her belly flipped as she careened closer and closer to the edge. She'd forgotten how deeply committed the man was to cunnilingus. He went for it without hesitation.

Every. Fucking. Time.

He never dialed it in. Instead, he got off on it as much as she did. Like there was nothing more important in his world than bringing her to ecstasy.

"OhmygodOhmygodOhmygod... YES!"

Fireworks exploded behind her tightly closed eyelids. She dug her heels in, trying to get a reprieve from the pleasure rocketing through her body. Her legs quivered as she arched her back. She was breathless and dizzy.

"That's my girl." Darius pressed soft, warm kisses to her inner thigh. Then he trailed them up her body.

He kissed her shoulder and her neck, then whispered in her ear, "There is something so goddamn gratifying about that rapturous expression on your face when you're right there on the brink."

Audra felt giddy, then emotional, then a little angry.

She'd been his. She'd dreamed of someday being his wife, of sharing this passion and chemistry and affection for the rest of their lives. But he'd destroyed everything they'd built because he hadn't trusted her with his truth. Hadn't had enough faith in her to believe that she'd choose him.

"What's wrong, babe?" Darius furrowed his brows as he studied her face. He seemed to sense the sudden tension in her body.

"Nothing," Audra whispered.

Talking about it right now would only fuel the hurt and anger that simmered beneath the surface.

She kissed his mouth, tangy with a hint of her own essence. Cradling his cheek, she glided her pierced tongue against his.

Darius slipped his fingers into her hair, angling her head to deepen their kiss until they were both breathless. His thick, hard shaft teased her entrance.

He rolled off her suddenly, then returned from the bathroom with a strip of condoms. He ripped one open and sheathed himself.

Something in his ravenous gaze made her heart expand. She remembered the first time he looked at her that way. It was the night he'd first told her he loved her.

Darius gripped the base of his length and eased himself inside her, evoking a quiet gasp from her.

The connection between them was deeply satisfying. She'd craved his touch, his kiss. He pressed his mouth to hers, as he inched his way inside of her, stretching her body as it welcomed his again.

Audra sucked in a deep breath when he hit bottom. The friction of his body grinding against the already sensitive bundle of nerves brought her closer to the edge with every thrust until she shattered, clutching his strong biceps and calling his name.

He kissed her neck, his strokes harder and faster. His harsh whisper warmed her cheek. "God, I've missed you, Audra."

Her eyes suddenly burned with tears.

Darius tensed, then trembled. He fell onto his back beside her, both of them breathing heavily.

Neither of them spoke, and the awkward silence between them amplified every other sound. The tick of the wall clock. The roar of a passing motorcycle. The quiet whir of the warm air blowing through an overhead vent. The pounding of her own pulse.

Audra silently wiped away the tears that streaked her flaming cheeks.

She was beyond embarrassed.

Crying during sex? Really?

She'd never done that before. Not ever. No matter how great the sex was. And she knew better than to fall for the sweet nothings a man whispered while on the verge. In that moment of orgasm-induced, temporary insanity, he'd promise you the world.

No one should be held to the things they uttered on the verge of carnal bliss.

So why had she been so touched by Darius's simple admission?

Audra discreetly wiped away the warm tears that leaked from the corners of her eyes as the truth hit her.

She'd been moved by Darius's words because he'd expressed exactly what she was feeling.

She'd missed him, too. In a way she hadn't missed any other man. Because she'd loved him like she'd loved no other.

No matter how much she tried to deny it, the truth was she still loved Darius. And she wanted him in her life.

The man you want isn't necessarily the man you need, Audra.

Her mother's words echoed in her head. She'd always trotted out that phrase whenever Audra was interested in someone who didn't quite fit her mother's plans for her. Which was why she'd hesitated to introduce her parents to Darius back then.

But maybe her mother was right.

She wanted Darius, but she needed a partner she could count on. Someone who trusted her implicitly. But there was something Darius was hiding from her still. She'd sensed it that day at the diner. And she sensed it now.

She'd given in to desire. Given him her body. Taken his. But she would never again give her heart to a man who couldn't be trusted with it.

Fourteen

Darius's heart thudded in his chest, his breathing labored as he came down from the incredible high of being with Audra again.

Making love to her was even better than he remembered. So much so that he'd told her how much he'd missed her.

Every word he'd spoken was true. He just hadn't intended to say them. Especially not in the heat of passion.

He'd seen the glint of tears in her eyes. Was it because she believed him or because she didn't?

Either way, things now felt awkward between them. Both of them likely embarrassed by their outbursts of emotion.

Darius rolled onto his side. He pressed a soft kiss to her lips and stroked her cheek. "You were incredible, Audra."

She glided her fingertips down his side. "So were you."

Darius kissed her again and excused himself. In the restroom, he splashed cold water on his face.

Just take it easy. Everything will be fine.

Who was he kidding? Everything was *not* fine. He'd finally cleared the air with Audra about what had happened back then. But now here he was forced to keep another truth from her.

He couldn't even consider getting serious with Audra until he could tell her everything. Why he'd really been summoned to Royal. What his connection was to the Blackwoods. But he couldn't do that until he'd talked to his mother and stepfather.

He'd fly home today to talk to them, if that were possible. But they were still on the twenty-one-day tour of Europe they'd always dreamed about. They wouldn't be back until after his show.

When he returned to the bedroom, Audra was gone, and the bedroom door was open. He put on his boxers and trekked through the house to find her in the office. She was in her panties and bra, bending to retrieve the dress they'd discarded there earlier.

"You're not leaving, are you?" He leaned against the doorframe.

"It's late, and we've both had a really long day." She sunk her teeth gently into her lower lip when her gaze dropped below his waist momentarily. Her cheeks flushed and she redirected her gaze, as if she hadn't seen him in a lot less moments before. "Besides, you probably have an early morning planned."

Darius looped an arm around her waist. He tipped her chin so her eyes met his. "Stay. Please."

Her breath hitched at his soft plea. "I shouldn't. It'd be weird."

"Only if we allow it to be." He shrugged. "Besides, you promised to model those swimsuits for me."

She laughed nervously, leaning into him rather than pulling away. "I believe what I promised was an honest opinion."

"How can you do that if you don't try it on?"

"I suppose you're right. And a promise is a promise."

She laid the dress across a chair and grabbed the one-piece swimming suit.

"The deconstructed one-shoulder design is gorgeous. It's both modest and sexy with all of this sheer detailing." She held it up to the light. "And the solid fabric isn't so thin that it's transparent." Audra turned the suit around, laying it across his desk. She trailed her fingers over the back. "Premium fabric, well made, thoughtfully designed, and it's my favorite color."

"Eggplant," he chimed in, chuckling when they said it simultaneously. He shrugged at her look of surprise. "What? How could I forget that? I've never met another person whose favorite color was eggplant."

Audra fought back the smile that lit her eyes. She checked the label inside. "Did you really order this in my size? How'd you know?"

"I am a clothing designer," he reminded her. "I've gotten pretty good at guesstimating a woman's measurements. I'll grab a bottle of wine while you try the suit on. Red or white?"

"White." The tension seemed to melt from her shoulders. She no longer seemed anxious to leave.

Darius leaned in and kissed her cheek. "Be right back."

He found his shorts and shirt and got dressed before returning to the kitchen to throw together a quick charcuterie and cheese tray. He opened a bottle of chardonnay and grabbed two wineglasses, slipping the stems into the designated notches on the board.

When he returned to the office, Audra spun slowly, giving him a good look at the suit from all sides.

"What do you think?" She beamed, one fist propped on her hip.

"Wow." He set the tray down and rubbed his chin as he assessed the fit of the suit. "You look incredible, Audra. Even more so than I imagined when I designed it for you."

She cocked her head. "You designed the suit for me?"

Suddenly, he couldn't seem to keep his mouth shut. "I designed it with your body type in mind."

"In my favorite color and size." She approached him with an incredulous grin that made her eyes twinkle.

"Wine?" He handed her a glass, then took a seat in front of the desk, not responding to her implication.

Audra flashed a teasing smile, then sipped her wine. Setting her glass down, she plucked a few kalamata olives and a square of French Gruyère cheese from the tray. She popped them in her mouth, then strode around the room in the suit.

She turned to look down at the back of the suit, her body slightly twisted. "I like the way this one provides full coverage in the back." She bent over and touched her toes, her dark brown hair falling forward.

Yep. Definitely a fan of that new, curvier ass.

God bless every pint of ice cream, donut, cookie and latte that had contributed to it over the past five years.

Darius adjusted himself in the chair and crossed one ankle over his opposite knee.

"And I love that it stays put. It doesn't ride up when you bend or stretch." Audra ran her fingers through her hair and grabbed a couple of red grapes from the tray. "Should I try on the bikini now?"

God, yes.

"If you wouldn't mind," he said nonchalantly, without looking up from the tray where he was spreading chèvre on a cracker and topping it with prosciutto.

Audra left the room with the bikini in her hand.

He'd just seen every inch of her, up close and personal. Yet he was practically hyperventilating at the thought of seeing her in that bikini.

He was a complete goner.

Audra returned in a few minutes, wearing the two-piece garment. He nearly choked on his prosciutto and cracker.

She patted his back and handed him his glass of wine as he coughed and sputtered.

Smooth, playa. Really smooth.

"Are you all right?" She stood over him, her warm brown eyes assessing him as she tried to hold back a grin.

"Fine." He drank more wine. "Promise."

Audra strutted to the middle of the room and turned slowly so he could see the bikini from every angle. "That reaction... I'm not sure if that means I look really bad in the suit or—"

"You look amazing. Trust me." He walked toward her but stopped a few feet shy. Arms folded, he propped his chin on his fist and studied the fit of the suit and the give of the fabric as she moved. "How do you feel in it?"

"I really like this one, too," she said. "It says it's the same size, but it fits more snugly. It doesn't have full coverage in the back, like the first one did. But it doesn't show so much skin that I feel self-conscious."

"May I?" He reached toward her.

"After what happened earlier?" Audra's cheeks flushed. "I should think so."

"It's become habit, I suppose. I always ask permission if I need to touch one of the models." He adjusted the band just below her bust. "Do the ties feel secure?" He rested his fingertips on her waistline, just above the ties at her hips.

Audra stared at him for a moment, her gaze heated. She looped her arms around his neck and lifted onto her toes.

"Why don't we find out?" she asked in a soft, husky voice, moments before his mouth crashed against hers.

Darius pressed one hand flat to her back, the other gripped the firm, round globes that had sent his pulse racing.

He kissed her hungrily. As if they hadn't made love less than an hour ago. In response, she clutched his shirt, pulling him closer. Seemingly as desperate for the connection as he was.

Darius lifted her, his hands planted firmly on her bottom. Audra wrapped her legs around him.

They both groaned a little at the sensation of his hardened length surging against the warm space between her thighs.

Darius took a few steps backward until his calves hit the sofa behind him. He sank down with Audra straddling his lap. She dug her knees into the sofa on either side of him, as she worked her hips, sending a jolt of sensation up his spine and making his heart thump against his chest.

Darius tugged on the ribbon at the back of the bikini top, then loosened the ribbon at the back of her neck. Audra yanked the untethered material from between their bodies and dropped it onto the floor.

He kissed her hard, his pulse racing and his head spinning. Audra was the only woman who'd ever made him feel such a crazed desperation to kiss her. To touch her. To make love to her. As if nothing else mattered.

Audra grasped the bottom of his shirt and tugged it over his head. When she'd discarded the garment, Darius took her in his arms again.

He loved the feel of her naked breasts against his chest. He trailed his fingertips down her back with a light, feather touch, then gripped her hips as she moved against him, increasing the friction against her clit through the thin garments they wore.

Finally, he couldn't take another moment of the heat and desire building between them. He needed to be inside this incredible woman again.

He loosened the bow on each hip until the bikini bottom fell open. Audra shifted her weight to her knees, allowing him to lift his hips and slide his shorts and boxers off. He retrieved one of the condoms from the pocket of his shorts, where he'd, thankfully, had the presence of mind to stash them when he'd gotten dressed.

Darius ripped open the foil packet and sheathed himself. He grabbed the base of his length and pressed it against her slick opening, his other hand resting on her hip.

Audra's lashes fluttered as she slowly lowered herself onto him. Their bodies fit together as if the past five years apart had never existed.

She whimpered with pleasure, her head lolling to one side. He swept her hair off her neck and shoulder and planted kisses there. Then he placed his hands on her bottom, guiding her up and down his shaft.

Audra was getting closer. Her whimpers came louder and faster as their hips slammed together. She dug her fingers into his shoulders, her cries growing louder.

"Fuck, Audra." His voice trembled, his arousal building. "You feel so fucking good. I need you to come for me, baby. Because I don't know how much longer I can hold on."

Her eyes drifted shut and she slipped a hand between them, her fingers moving over her clit. Her movements, slow and deliberate at first, became quicker and more determined.

He'd always loved her uninhibited nature. She wasn't ashamed to ask for or take whatever she needed.

It was one of the sexiest things about her.

He tightened his grip on her hips as he glided her up and down on his painfully hard shaft. Her breathing was quick and shallow. Her whimpers loud and breathy. Finally, her body tensed, the muscles inside her quivering as she called out his name.

Darius laid her on the couch, his hips thrusting hard and fast and the pressure building until he shuddered, cursing and moaning, as he found his own release.

He kissed her, his heart racing as he tried to catch his breath.

"Don't go, Audra." Darius couldn't bear the thought of her leaving. He craved the warmth and comfort of falling asleep with her in his arms. The joy of waking to her lovely face and sweet smile. "Stay. Please."

She stroked his cheek and nodded. Her kiss-swollen lips quirked in a faint smile that made his heart feel full and reminded him of all the reasons he'd fallen in love with her back then.

The reasons he was falling for her all over again.

Later, they sat in bed drinking wine and nibbling from the charcuterie tray. He was glad she'd accepted his invitation to stay.

"Well, we know the bikini is easy to get in and out of." Her mouth curved in a mischievous grin. "I'll have to swim in it to see if it stays on as well as it comes off."

Darius chuckled, then pressed a kiss to her lips. "If you could swim in both suits, that'd be great. I'd love to see how they hold up to chlorine and a hand wash."

"Sure." She swiped some aged Gouda and a few grapes from the tray, nibbling on them. An uncomfortable silence settled over them again.

Darius set his wineglass down and turned to her. "Audra, we should probably talk about what's happened between us tonight."

"I disagree." She tucked some of her wavy hair behind her ear. "I don't mean never," she clarified. "I just don't think either of us is prepared to have this discussion right now, while our emotions are still high." She plucked another grape from the tray and chewed thoughtfully. "We should process what's happened and how we feel about it. So neither of us makes any promises we aren't prepared to keep."

Her voice was calm, her reasoning cerebral and

dispassionate. The very opposite of the woman who'd clawed her way up his body not an hour before.

"Are you sure that's what you want, Audra?" He threaded their fingers.

"Of course." She pressed her lips into a smile and nodded once. "We're both really involved in our work right now. I'm racing to make sure all of Sophie and Nigel's pieces are completed on time and to their satisfaction. You've got the biggest event of your career coming up in less than a week. I don't want this to become a distraction…for either of us."

"Okay." Darius kissed her hand, his eyes not leaving hers. "Then we'll revisit this conversation—"

"After LA Fashion Week and Sophie and Nigel's wedding." She shrugged. "That's just a few weeks. If this is really something worth exploring, a few weeks of contemplation won't hurt."

"Right," Darius agreed with more conviction than he felt. He snatched a few grapes from the tray. "In the meantime, maybe you'll let me take you out to dinner in town."

"As your friend and neighbor?" she asked, her eyes searching his.

"As the woman I'm dating…or whatever this is that we're doing." He pressed a lingering kiss to her mouth.

"Dare, I don't know if it's wise for us to take this beyond these walls."

He was surprised that she used the nickname she'd always called him. It didn't even seem like a conscious decision. Just something that had slipped out. But that didn't soften the impact of her words.

They were five years older, both successful entrepreneurs. Yet, their relationship had regressed. Now she wasn't just hiding him from her disapproving parents. She wanted him to be her dirty little secret.

"We should decide on our next steps, based purely on what we want," she continued. "The fewer people involved in that conversation, the better."

"You mean Sophie." Darius swept back the hair that fell over one eye when she nodded and tucked it behind her ear. He kissed her. "If you really want to hide out here in my bed, I think I could be okay with that. For now."

"Oh, you're taking me out all right, big shot." She stroked his stubbled chin. "But for now, if anyone asks, we're just friends. Deal?"

"Deal." He moved the tray onto the floor. Then he pulled her closer and kissed her.

Audra wasn't prepared to decide whether this was a meaningless fling or destiny. He could pretend that was fine by him. But he was clear on how he felt.

He'd made a colossally boneheaded mistake when he'd walked away from her, and he'd been given a second chance. He wouldn't blow it.

Besides, two weeks would give him time to tell his parents that he now knew Buckley Blackwood was his father. So when he and Audra finally talked, he could tell her everything.

Lies and half-truths would never come between them again.

Fifteen

Audra had spent most of the past three days either in bed with Darius or working quietly beside him in his office or by the pool.

He'd taken her out to dinner nearly every night. They'd gone to the Glass House—an upscale farm-to-table restaurant, and the Silver Saddle—a bar and tapas restaurant. Both were located in the Bellamy, Royal's five-star resort, inspired by the lavish Biltmore estate in Asheville, North Carolina.

They'd also shared a casual meal at the place that had first brought them together: Royal Diner.

But with just a few days left to prepare for the runway show, Darius needed to get back to California to be onsite. He'd made love to her that morning, kissed her goodbye then left her naked and sated in his bed.

Audra slept in an extra hour, then climbed out of bed

and put on the Thr3d bikini that Darius had designed just for her. He'd had a second made more precisely to her measurements than the first. It fit perfectly. She went to the kitchen to grab a glass of juice before her morning swim when she saw Darius's thoughtful gift.

There was a gorgeous bouquet of two dozen red roses in a clear glass vase with a lovely note that made her smile. Another two dozen pink roses were on the coffee table in the family room with another sweet note apologizing for not being able to be there. Later, when she went to the bathroom to grab a towel, she discovered another two dozen roses, only these were white. The card read: *Can't wait to see you again. So come join me. If you do, I have a special surprise for you.*

Audra couldn't help the grin that spread from ear to ear. She regarded herself in the bathroom mirror. She looked like a giddy schoolgirl who'd fallen head over heels in love.

And maybe she had. Because Audra couldn't imagine going back to life without him.

But even if she could get over their past and her nagging suspicions that there was something he wasn't telling her, there were additional obstacles they'd need to address.

The Audra Lee Covington brand headquarters was in Dallas. Thr3d was based in Los Angeles. And they were both obsessed with their businesses. Could they make time for a long-distance relationship once they'd returned to their everyday lives? Was that what either of them wanted?

Then there were her parents.

Darius hadn't been wrong believing that her parents would've disapproved of their relationship. He wasn't

from a wealthy, powerful or political family. None of
that had mattered to her then. Nor did it matter now.
She hoped her parents would be impressed that Darius
had built Thr3d from nothing.

If they couldn't respect her choice, it would put a
further strain on her relationship with them. But she
didn't need their money or their approval. She and her
eponymous business could survive without either. Still,
she'd be much happier if her parents could accept her
relationship with Darius.

"You're getting way ahead of yourself. There is no
relationship," she muttered, removing the silk scarf she
slept in and smoothing down her hair, pineappled in a
wavy ponytail near the front of her head. She released
her hair and slipped the tie onto her wrist until she got
ready to get into the pool.

Her phone rang and she glanced down at it.

Cash again.

Audra sighed. She realized that Cash's pride was
wounded when she'd broken things off with him. But
she'd done so as kindly as possible. They'd known each
other for so long, and their families were close. She
hadn't wanted to hurt him or create tension between
their parents.

Cash was a good guy. He cared about the community and championed a number of worthy causes. She
respected him, and she believed he'd someday accom-
plish great things. But she just didn't love him in that
way, and she realized now that she never would.

But Cash was obviously still determined to win her
back.

That was why she'd eagerly accepted Sophie and
Nigel's proposal to spend time in Royal. And she was

glad she had. It'd given her a chance to clear her head. Reminded her of what a healthy, happy relationship looked like. And maybe, just maybe, she would get her happily-ever-after with Darius, after all.

Audra had been on the phone all day. She'd fielded calls from her design team, last-minute requests from clothing designers showing at LA Fashion Week, and an actress and her musician husband who wanted to borrow pieces for a movie premiere.

She was physically and mentally exhausted. And famished.

Audra was back at her own rental home, and she'd worked through lunch to take a call with a West Coast designer.

She made herself a grilled cheese sandwich on artisan bread with smoked provolone, prosciutto, caramelized onions and heirloom tomatoes. Then she dove back into working on the engagement ring and wedding band designs for another couple.

Her phone rang again.

It was Sophie. Audra sighed. She adored Sophie and Nigel, but if Sophie made one more change or special request for their rings or custom bridal party gifts, Audra was going to scream.

"Hey, Sophie. What's up?"

"Audra, I'm glad I caught you. The *Secret Lives* ladies invited me to join them for a girls' night out before the wedding. I've invited a few friends. You should join us."

"I don't know, Sophie," Audra studied the ring design on her tablet. She wasn't satisfied with it. "I'll probably be working late."

"You and Darius are workaholics. You can't work around the clock. Besides, taking a little break will give you a fresh perspective. I do it all the time."

Audra's mouth twisted as she studied the design. Sophie was right, she needed to step away from it for a few hours and come back with fresh eyes.

"This isn't another setup, is it?" Audra paced the floor. "If so, hard pass."

"It isn't. I promise. It'll just be me, the girls, a couple of cameras and a few million viewers." Sophie laughed. "Free publicity for my brand and yours. Are you really going to say no to that?"

She has a point. "Where?"

"The Glass House. Have you been there?"

Audra glanced at the three vases overflowing with roses that she'd brought back to her place, thinking of the dinner she and Darius had there a couple nights before. "Yes."

"Perfect. Then you know where it is. Get dolled up and meet us there at seven thirty. My friends are a hoot. This is going to be tons of fun, I promise."

Audra agreed and ended the call with Sophie.

A girls' night out might be nice. Most of her friends lived in New York or LA, so she hadn't had many girls' nights since moving to Dallas. She'd focused on work and growing the Audra Lee Covington brand. She had no regrets about that. Still, it'd been nice spending time with Sophie and Darius in Royal.

It almost felt like she had a social life again.

She'd gone to plenty of functions while she and Cash dated, but they were usually stuffy fund-raisers at country clubs and the homes of wealthy donors. Not the kind of place where she could cut loose and be herself.

Audra turned off her tablet and went to the closet to find something to wear. She was actually looking forward to a night out with Sophie and her friends.

Audra stepped out of her convertible and into the lobby of the Glass House.

"Audra, I'm glad you made it," Sophie practically squealed. "You already know Tessa Bateman and Milan Valez. Meet the rest of my friends."

Sophie introduced her to Shelby Mackenzie; Sophie's new sister-in-law, Irina Blackwood, who was expecting; Rachel Galloway; Lydia Harris, whose husband, James, was the current president of the Texas Cattleman's Club; Alexis Slade-Clayton; and Dixie Musgraves, who owned both her rental home and the ranch where she and Darius had kissed.

Then there were the *Secret Lives* ladies: Rafaela Marchesi, Lulu Shepard, Seraphina Martinez, who was engaged to a local man and would be leaving the show at the end of the season, and Zooey Kostas. Miranda Dupree Blackwood—Sophie's ex-stepmother, to whom her father had left his fortune—was notably absent.

"A few others might join us later, but the majority of us are here. We're just waiting for the camera crew to get everything set up in the room," Sophie informed her.

One of the producers of the show announced they were ready, and the hostess asked them to follow her to a private dining room.

Audra froze. She could swear she heard someone call her name. *It can't be.* She turned around.

It definitely was.

"What are you doing in Royal?"

"Looking for you, of course." Her ex, Cash, gave her a bright smile, his hazel eyes twinkling.

Audra looked over at the group of women who were staring in their direction with interest.

"I'll catch up with you shortly," she said with an overly cheerful voice.

She didn't do drama or messiness. As the daughter of a politician, it was something that had been drilled into her head as a little girl.

Smile for the cameras. You can fall apart once you're alone in your room.

With the *Secret Lives* cast and crew onsite, the last thing she needed was for them to get wind of possible drama between the diamond heiress and her ex, the aspiring politician. The headline practically wrote itself.

Out of either concern or curiosity, the women hadn't moved.

"Cash is a family friend. We've known each other since we were five. It's fine, I promise." That seemed to convince them.

Audra turned back to her ex, her smile gone. "Did you follow me here?"

"Yes, but not in a creepy way." He ran a hand through his dark blond hair and chuckled. "I went to the house where you've been staying. You were pulling out of the driveway, so I followed you here."

"How did you know where I'm staying?" She propped a hand on her hip.

"Your mother told me. I was concerned because you haven't been answering my calls."

Audra was going to have to have a talk with her mother.

"Well, as you can see, I'm fine, Cash. You shouldn't have come here. Good night." She turned to walk away.

"Audra, wait. Since I'm here, let me treat you to dinner."

"I already have plans."

"Then I won't keep you long. Maybe we could just have a quick coffee?" Cash smiled in that disarming way he employed with complaining constituents and opposing lawmakers.

Audra sighed. She glanced around the lobby, hoping no one recognized either of them. "Thirty minutes, Cash."

"That's more than enough time to say what I came to say." A broad smile spread across his handsome face, revealing his perfectly white teeth.

"Is everything all right, Audra?" Sophie approached suddenly and slipped her arm through Audra's. She eyed Cash as if she was trying to place his face. "We're starting soon."

"Sophie Blackwood, right?" He grinned.

"That's right." Sophie frowned. "Do we know each other?"

"State Representative Cassius Johannsson." He extended his hand and shook hers. "And sadly, Audra's ex." He kept his tone and expression light.

"Oh." Sophie's gaze shifted from Cash's to hers, then back again. "And how do you know me?"

"I worked with your father in the past." His tone became more solemn. "He was extremely proud of you, Sophie. I'm very sorry for your family's loss. I know your father could be a tough old guy, but we worked on a lot of important projects together. He's done more good than you probably know."

"Thank you, Representative Johannsson." Sophie seemed more perturbed than comforted by the man's words. She raked her fingers through her dark hair. "What brings you to Royal?"

"Call me Cash. All my friends do." He smiled warmly as he smoothed the lapels of his impeccable navy suit. He nodded toward Audra. "I'm sorry to interfere with your plans for the evening, but I need to speak with Audra for a few minutes. You'll hardly notice she's gone."

"We're just going to have coffee and a quick chat over at the bar," Audra assured her. "Don't wait for me to order, but I'll be there as soon as I can."

Audra forced a smile so her new friend wouldn't worry. Cash was harmless, if overly persistent. It was the politician in him. Win or lose, the campaign was never really over.

Sophie nodded, then turned to leave.

Audra turned to Cash, her arms folded. "Did you really need to tell her we dated?"

"It's true." He shrugged; his eyes suddenly filled with sadness. "And it's certainly not something I'm trying to hide."

He'd loved her, and she'd broken his heart. The least she could do was have a cup of coffee with him and make her intentions clear.

Sixteen

Audra and Cash sat at the bar. She ordered coffee and he ordered braised beef sliders, parmesan vegetable fritters and a Sazerac—his preferred drink.

"You're sure I can't get you a Sex on the Beach?" Cash turned on his stool to face her.

"No, thank you. I'd much rather talk about why you followed me here."

"Isn't it obvious?" He laid a gentle hand on her forearm. "I miss you, Audra."

She didn't respond right away. What could she say that she hadn't said before?

"I know things weren't perfect between us, Audra. Being a public servant is a demanding job. Surely, you understand that. Your father has been an elected official most of your life."

"I do understand. But your career isn't the issue,

Cash. I'm fond of you, but I just don't feel the same way about you that you do about me." Audra thanked the bartender when he set her coffee in front of her. She added sugar and cream.

"Maybe not right now, but if you'd only give it a little more time…" He stroked her forearm with his thumb, a soothing technique he'd employed whenever she was upset. "You'd realize how good we are together."

Audra withdrew her arm from his grasp. "We're just not compatible romantically. You're a good man, Cash, but we want very different things from life. Isn't it better that we figured that out now? I want a relationship that makes me happy, and I want the same for you."

She picked up her cup and sipped her coffee.

"Is that what you've found with that Thr3d guy you've been seen all over town with?"

Audra nearly spilled her coffee. She slammed the mug down. It clanked against the saucer.

"You've been following me?"

"I spent the past few hours in town. When I mentioned that we were longtime friends, the locals couldn't wait to tell me about the guy you've been spending so much time with. The guy you're living next door to." He emphasized the last sentence, indicating that he suspected there was something going on between her and Darius.

She had no wish to deny it. Nor would she apologize for being a grown-ass, unattached woman living her best life. But she'd been the one who'd insisted on keeping their relationship secret.

If anyone asks, we're just friends.

But there were no restrictions on sharing their past. "We dated in grad school. But renting homes next door to each other in Royal is purely coincidence, as crazy as it might seem."

It was the truth, and yet it sounded impossible, even to her.

"Either way, it's none of your business. Nor is it anyone else's," she added, in case he planned to run back to her mother with news of her suspected fling.

"Our relationship ended less than three months ago, Audra. I'm worried this guy is taking advantage of you at a vulnerable point in your life."

"I broke it off with you, remember?"

"I know, but…" He gripped his glass. "I assumed this was a phase you needed to go through. That you'd eventually realize how well matched we are."

"I don't want to be *well matched*, Cash. I want to be totally, completely, unapologetically in love."

"We were happy together, Audra. And our parents were happy for us. They've been hoping we'd get together our entire lives."

"But I wasn't happy. Or does that not matter to any of you?"

Cash took a healthy sip of his Sazerac; a sure sign his patience was wearing thin. A tendency he shared with her father.

"How much do you know about this guy, Audra?"

She frowned, her forehead tensing. He'd hit a nerve. And from the calculating expression on his face, Cash knew it, too.

"I know enough. So stop prying. What I do and whom I do it with is none of your affair. Nor is it my parents'."

"We're concerned. That's all."

"I thank you for your concern. But go home. I'm fine, and I'll deal with my parents tomorrow."

"Don't be so hard on them." He tapped a finger on the bar. "They're just trying to protect you."

She'd had about enough of his condescension.

"I love my parents, but I'm tired of everything I do being weighed by its political merits first. The schools I attended, whether or not I pledged a sorority and which one. What career I chose. I've had enough of it. And I've had enough of this."

She sat taller, steeling her spine as she fixed her gaze on his. "It's over, Cash. I'd like to believe we can still be friends, but I have nothing more to offer you."

"Audra, you don't mean that."

"Yes, I do." She placed a hand over his on the bar. As angry as she was with Cash, she didn't relish hurting him.

"Don't you want to be with someone who truly adores you? Because, as your friend, that's what I want for you. It's what you deserve. But I can't give that to you."

He looked as if she'd cleaved his heart with an arrow. "You said I wasn't romantic enough. So I thought I'd come down here and surprise you. Show you that I can be the man you want."

"You shouldn't have to change who you are, and I'd never expect you to." Audra checked the time on her phone. She leaned in and kissed his cheek. "Goodbye, Cash. Give my regards to your parents and have a safe trip back to Dallas."

Audra walked toward the private room where Sophie and her friends were waiting. She didn't know what would become of the relationship she was forging with

Darius. But she knew one thing for sure. She wouldn't settle for a relationship with Cash.

She didn't love him. Not in the way he deserved to be loved. And he certainly wasn't capable of providing her with the passion and companionship she enjoyed with Darius.

Her cheeks tightened in an involuntary smile as she wondered what Darius was doing now.

Before she'd arrived tonight, she hadn't decided whether to accept Darius's invitation to his show. But now she was sure. She was counting the days until they'd be together again.

Seventeen

Darius had been running all day. He was sure he hadn't slept more than three hours a night since he'd returned home. A direct contrast to the sound sleep he'd been getting with Audra in his arms back in Royal.

He was tired, cranky, and now that he thought of it, he was hungry.

"Did I eat today?" he asked his assistant, Anastasia Winters.

"Not unless you're counting that gum you've been chewing for the past hour." She pushed up the cuff of her sweater revealing one of two elaborate tattoo sleeves. This one dominated by vibrant greens, blues and aqua.

"Have *you* eaten?" he asked.

She gave him an even dirtier look.

"God, I'm sorry." He stood, rubbing a hand over his

head. "I vowed to myself that I'd never be that boss. We should get something. Why don't you order in? Your choice."

Anastasia grinned. "Then we're ordering from my favorite steak house. Want your usual?"

"That's fine." He settled back in his chair.

"Sounds like I arrived just in time." Audra was standing in the doorway, patting her stomach. "I'm starving and I could go for a good steak."

"Audra." Darius stood, making his way across the room.

She hadn't responded either way to his invitation to join him in Los Angeles for the show and he'd assumed she hadn't planned to come.

He hugged her tightly, lifting her off her feet. He whispered in her ear, "This is an amazing surprise."

She looked incredible in a simple red dress that grazed her thighs, a fitted, waist-length leather jacket and a sexy pair of cutout peep-toe heels.

He could already envision the entire outfit piled on the floor beside his bed. On second thought, the heels would stay on.

Darius put her down, his hand pressed to her cheek. He wanted so badly to kiss her, but they'd agreed to take this slowly and play it cool in public.

Anastasia cleared her throat.

"Oh, I'm sorry. Audra, this is my assistant, Anastasia Winters. Stasia, this is my friend from grad school—"

"You went to grad school with Audra Lee Covington? You never mentioned that. Wow, boss, talk about burying the lede." She stepped forward, wiping her hands on her blue jeans and sifting her fingers through her blond hair streaked with shades of purple, pink and aqua.

Stasia looked starstruck as she extended her hand to Audra. "Hello, Ms. Covington, it's such a pleasure to meet you. Your jewelry designs are absolutely amazing."

"Thank you, Anastasia. Please, call me Audra. And it's a pleasure to meet you, too. I've heard a lot about you. Darius thinks quite highly of you."

"I feel the same. I give him a hard time, but he's an amazing boss and Thr3d is a fantastic company. I'm lucky to work here."

"You're not just saying that because I'm treating you to lunch, are you?" Darius teased.

"You're treating me to lunch because I'm an amazing assistant and you'd be lost without me." Stasia grinned, then studied the two of them for a moment. "You know, I could use some fresh air. I think I'll walk over there and eat. How about I bring something back for the two of you in—" she checked her watch "—about an hour. The menu is in the file in your desk. Just let me know what you want."

"I can wait an hour. How about you, Audra?" Darius asked.

"Sounds good to me." She put her purse down and started to take off her jacket.

Darius slipped it from Audra's shoulders and hung it on a nearby hook. "Perfect. I'll call you in thirty minutes. Be sure to grab the corporate—"

"Credit card?" Stasia waved it in front of him, then slipped it into her back pocket. "I'm on it. I'll be gone for an hour, and I'll make sure everyone else knows not to bother you. I already set your phone to Do Not

Disturb." She gave him a knowing look and pulled the door closed. "Goodbye, you two."

"Sorry about that." Darius sat behind his desk. "I never said anything to Stasia about us, I swear."

She stood in front of him. "I'm pretty sure that reception you gave me was what clued her in."

"Maybe I could've dialed back a little," he conceded. "But I showed admirable restraint, given how incredible you look in that dress."

"Do I?" She smoothed the garment down over her hips.

"You do." Darius pulled Audra closer. She pressed her warm lips to his clean-shaven head, then sat on his lap.

There was something comforting about the woman who believed in his dream from the beginning being there on the eve of the biggest moment of his career. Everything seemed to slow down, and for the first time in days, he could catch his breath.

Audra seemed just as happy to see him.

He kissed her, the kiss slowly building in intensity. His fingers dug into the smooth, toasted-brown skin of her thighs and itched to glide beneath the red fabric and bury his fingers in the wet heat between her strong thighs.

Admirable restraint indeed.

Audra pulled away, one hand to his cheek. She smiled. "Good thing I wore the nontransferable lipstick today."

"I guess it is." He kissed her again. "You should've told me you were coming in today. I would've picked you up from the airport. Where's your luggage?"

"Downstairs. I came straight here. I haven't even checked into my hotel yet."

"Don't. Stay at my place. I'll take you out there now."

"All the way out to Pasadena? With traffic it'll take you forever to go all the way out there and come back. I'll take a car service instead."

"Are you sure? I don't mind." For Audra, he'd make the time. The show was just two days away, but his team was more than capable of handling everything. He was a perfectionist, and his obsession with getting every detail right was in overdrive.

She kissed him again, her hand pressed to his chest. "I'm positive." She leaned in and whispered in his ear. "Besides, the sooner you're done here, the sooner I'll see you back at your place."

"I can't disagree with your logic," he said, his voice faint.

He picked up his cell phone and tapped out a message. "There. I just sent my address and the code to get inside the house. Will you at least stay for lunch?"

"Sure, if you have the time."

"Good. I'll call Stas with our lunch orders and then give you a tour of the place."

"Thought you'd never ask." She smiled. "I'd love to see it."

"There's one more thing I want to ask." He hesitated. "I'd love it if you'd model one of the swimsuits in the show."

"On the runway? You can't be serious." She paced the floor beside his desk. "Whatever tall, thin, leggy glamazon you hired to walk the runway in the suit will look far better in it than me."

"I disagree." He stood, too, and wrapped his arms

around her waist, stilling her. "You forget that I've already seen you in it. I designed those swimsuits for you, and you looked absolutely stunning in them."

"When do you need an answer?"

"By tomorrow at five."

She stroked his cheek. "Let me think about it. I'll let you know by then."

They called their lunch orders in to Stasia, and he showed her the fall lineup. After lunch, he gave her a tour of Thr3d's headquarters. Then he ordered a car service to take her to his house in Pasadena.

As he watched her leave, he knew two things.

First, as soon as the show was over, he'd tell his parents that he knew Buckley Blackwood was his biological father.

Second, as soon as his parents knew the truth, he'd tell Audra everything. And he'd introduce Audra to his mother and Will.

Eighteen

Audra tipped the driver and closed the door behind her. She slipped off her heels and padded through the large, beautiful, modern two-story home.

Darius Taylor-Pratt had certainly done well for himself. The home itself was gorgeous, and Audra could tell that it had been professionally decorated.

Every painting, every vase, every little knickknack was simply perfect.

It was the kind of inviting space one would hardly want to leave. And yet Darius had.

He'd been in Royal for several weeks. And she got the feeling that even when he was in LA, he spent most of his time at the office.

Audra took in the open space and light, bright modern decor. Initially, she'd been reluctant to accept Darius's invitation to stay with him. That's why she'd booked a hotel. But now she was glad she was here. It felt good to get to know this part of him.

Earlier, she'd been given a tour of his business and got to meet several of his employees. And now she was getting to see the space he called home.

She felt closer to him. As if she had gotten a few more of the missing puzzle pieces that comprised the complicated man she was falling for all over again.

She walked through the house and accessed the back patio. The outdoor space was lovely, and the pool was much bigger than the one at his rental in Royal.

She couldn't wait to hop in later. But for now, she needed a quick nap before heading out to her first client meeting.

Many of her clients lived in LA. Actors, pop stars, athletes, corporate heiresses, socialites, fashion designers and more. She spent a lot of time in LA icing the biggest names on the red carpet—even if their jewelry pieces were loaned, rather than purchased.

Establishing boutiques in Los Angeles and New York, where the bulk of her clients resided, was the next step in her ten-year business plan. A flagship boutique in Los Angeles or New York would expedite the growth of the Audra Lee Covington brand.

She hoped to squeeze in a few real estate appointments to test out the feasibility of buying space here. Maybe after the runway show, Darius would be willing to accompany her.

Audra made her way to the master bedroom, slipped out of the dress Darius had loved so much and crawled under the covers that still smelled like him.

Darius dragged himself into the house well after nine that evening. The downstairs space was dark except for the glow of the candles on the kitchen counter and on the dining room table.

The scent of the candles wafted through the space along with the savory scent of food. There were bags from one of his favorite restaurants in the trash.

She'd ordered dinner for them and he'd missed it.

They'd been running a mock runway show, still trying to iron out the run of show and the music selections. He'd let time get away from him. By the time he'd thought to call Audra, he hadn't gotten an answer.

"Audra," he called up the stairs. "Are you here?"

He went up the stairs and followed the sound of splashing water. He leaned against the doorframe and grinned. "There you are, beautiful. I'm sorry I missed dinner."

Audra was soaking in a tub filled with bubbles. A glorious, sweet scent filled the room.

"I understand how it is being a creative." She shrugged. "I'm just glad you made it home... I mean, to your home...when you did." Her cheeks flushed, as if she'd been embarrassed by saying *home*, as if they lived there together.

But it had given him a sense of warmth and comfort. Made him entertain the idea of coming home to Audra every day.

She sat up, the water sloshing. "I hope you don't mind that I used your tub."

"Not at all," he stepped inside the room and sat on the edge of the large garden tub. "I hardly use it. I'm more of a shower guy."

"Then you should join me." She grinned. "You've had a long, hard day. I'm sure you could use a relaxing soak."

She had a point; besides, he could hardly resist her

tempting offer, especially when she batted those beautiful brown eyes.

Darius stripped down and slipped into the tub behind her, wrapping her in his arms.

The warm water soothed his tired body and having her slick skin pressed to his was like a balm that calmed all the disquieting thoughts in his mind.

He relaxed against the back of the tub. His eyes drifted shut as he leaned his head against the wall.

"This *is* relaxing. I should do this more often."

"You should," she said. "It's a shame to have such a beautiful tub and barely use it. It's practically free therapy."

"Well, when you put it that way, how can I say no?" He kissed the side of her face. "Sorry I'm so late. We were practicing the runway lineup. Time got away from me."

Audra rested her arms atop his. "This is the biggest moment of your career. Of course, you want everything to be perfect. I realized when I came here that you'd be preoccupied with work. That's why I booked client appointments. I only returned a couple of hours ago myself."

"That's great." He was relieved she hadn't been knocking about the house bored while she waited for him. "Who'd you meet with?"

Audra rattled off the list of celebs and society folks and updated him on some of the appointments she had for the rest of the week. Many of them tastemakers and household names.

He squeezed her tight and kissed the side of her cheek. "I'm so incredibly proud of you, Audra. You've done everything you set out to do back when we were in grad school. Celebrities and royalty are beating down your door."

She glanced over her shoulder at him, a wide smile on her face. "Thanks. That means a lot. No one has ever said that to me. My dad was disappointed I didn't want to work for the family diamond business or go into politics. And my mother would be happier if I settled down with the 'right' man—" she used air quotes "—and became a society wife. But what I've done is nothing compared to what you've accomplished. You built Thr3d from nothing."

"Don't ever underestimate what you've accomplished, Audra. You followed your dream, despite the pressure from your parents to conform to their expectations. And you're incredibly talented. There's a reason A-listers are beating down your door."

She settled back against his chest. "Who knew that when we were plotting our dreams out five years ago that we'd both actually achieve them?"

He smiled fondly, recalling those lazy Sunday mornings when they'd sit in bed and plan their futures.

They'd both gotten exactly what they wanted; except he'd always planned that they'd do it together.

"How did your client meetings go?" he asked.

"Everything here went well."

"Did something happen in Royal?"

"I had an unexpected visitor. My ex, Cassius Johannsson. He's a Texas state representative. And our families have been friends for decades. We dated for a while, but I ended things three months ago."

"I see." Darius sucked in a quiet breath. "What did he want?"

"Me." She turned her body to face his and hugged

her knees. "He still has it in his head that I'll eventually come back to him."

"And how did you respond?" His heart raced.

"I told him that we're too different. I'm sorry my leaving hurt him, but it was the right thing for both of us." Audra smoothed back her hair. "I told him we could go back to being friends, but that's all I can offer him."

Darius could swear his heart leaped in his chest. Relieved, he pulled her into a passionate kiss.

Maybe Cash really was the better man. Maybe he deserved a woman like Audra more than Darius did. And maybe it made him selfish to want Audra for himself, but he did.

As soon as he could, he'd tell her everything. And this time, he wouldn't walk away.

After their bath, he took her to bed and made love to her. He held her in his arms as they drifted off to sleep after a late dinner and cocktails.

Audra rolled over to face him. She kissed him, then whispered, "I'll do it."

His brain was fuzzy, thanks to the combination of King's Finest bourbon, great sex and the promise of sound sleep.

"Fantastic, babe," he muttered, then added, "What is it that you're going to do?"

"I'll model the one-piece swimsuit in the show."

His brain woke up a little. "Are you sure?"

"My parents will probably freak," she said. "But yes. I want to do this. For you, but also for me."

He pulled her to him and cradled her in his arms. "I'll let the team know tomorrow. We won't announce that you'll be in the show. Instead, we'll say that we have a special guest appearing."

"Perfect." She seemed relieved.

She was perfect. She was everything he wanted. And he wouldn't blow this chance to have her back in his life again.

He just needed a few more days. Time to get through the show and for his parents to arrive back in town. Then he would confess everything to Audra and tell her he wanted to be with her, and only her.

Nineteen

Darius had been running all day on adrenaline and energy drinks. He was as terrified as he was excited by the fact that the show was beginning in minutes.

"Everyone take their places!" Stasia barked over her headset, and all of the models started to line up. A few of them still had a makeup artist or a hairstylist trailing behind them, adding final touches.

Stasia turned to him, cutting off the microphone. "You okay, boss? You look a little green."

"It's just the lighting. I'm fine." He narrowed his gaze at her. "Is the DJ ready to go?"

"Checked with him two minutes ago. He's ready whenever we are." She nodded behind him. "And so is she."

Before he could ask whom, Stasia had cut her microphone back on and was talking to a member of the lighting crew.

He turned in the direction she'd indicated just in time to see Audra.

"You look gorgeous." He leaned in and kissed her cheek, not wanting to ruin her lipstick.

"Thanks." Audra smoothed down the white, silk robe covering the eggplant-colored swimsuit. "How are you?"

"I'm fine." *Why does everyone keep asking that?* He must look as stressed as he felt. "Thanks for doing this. It's going to be an amazing finish to the show. Now you'd better go find your place in line before Stasia blows a gasket." He smiled.

"I will." She walked toward the queue, but then turned back to him. "Just take a deep breath. Everything is going to be fine. The collection is amazing, and buyers are going to be clamoring for it. You've outdone yourself, and I'm incredibly proud of you."

An involuntary smile spread across his face and a sense of calm descended over him. He nodded, thankful Audra was there.

Audra was right. The show had been amazing, and the swimwear had been a big hit, as had she. The crowd went crazy when they discovered that Audra Lee Covington was the special guest, modeling the swimsuit that was the pièce de résistance of the show.

Audra's pep talk had calmed him considerably. But it wasn't until he'd gone out onto the stage to thunderous applause, holding Audra's hand, that he'd taken his first full, deep breath all day.

Now as he stood on one of his favorite rooftop bars

in LA, surveying the skyline, he felt amazing. Almost like he was floating.

The rest of the team was scattered throughout the crowded after-party and Audra had gone to talk to a friend.

He glanced over to where she stood among a group of people taking center stage. Her magnificent, one-shoulder, gold lace dress had a dreamy layer of organza over the skirt. A high split over her right leg revealed miles of smooth, creamy brown skin. Her hair was still pulled up in the braided crown she'd worn during the show.

He couldn't wait to get her back home, all to himself.

"We're about to head out." Anastasia approached him, holding the hand of her girlfriend, May Chen. "We're both wiped out and I imagine you are, too."

"I am. I might sleep for two days after this." Darius took a pull of his bourbon, then set his glass down. "It goes without saying that I could never have done this without you. You're incredible." He hugged her. "Thank you for putting up with me."

"Same." She winked. "The show was amazing. We're already getting international orders for the collection. A few buyers want to know if they can order the swimwear for this summer."

It was something they'd anticipated and hoped for. A plan was in place to ensure delivery.

"Great to hear. Now get out of here and get some much-needed rest."

Anastasia and May turned to leave, but then Stasia whispered something to May and walked back to him.

"Look, boss, I can understand why you might not want to tell us how you feel about Audra, but I hope you haven't made the mistake of not telling *her* how you feel." They both glanced over to where Audra had dissolved into laughter.

A slow smile spread across his face. He picked up his glass and finished his bourbon. "Go," he said, one side of his mouth pulled into a smirk.

Stasia grinned. "Good night. See you Monday," she called over her shoulder as she grabbed May's hand and they disappeared into the crowd.

"So…" Audra was standing in front of him. "Are we going to another after-party or do I get to take my man home to bed?"

"Your man, huh?" He set his glass down. His heart beat faster as he took a few steps toward her and took her hands in his. "I like the sound of that."

She leaned toward him, her eyes drifting closed.

"You know there are gossip columnists and paparazzi still hanging around," he whispered, eyeing the crowd for cell phones or cameras pointed in their direction.

"I do, and I don't care." Her eyes were filled with a certainty that made his heart dance. "Now kiss me."

She didn't need to tell him twice.

He cradled her face and closed the space between them, pressing his lips to hers.

He was falling in love with this woman all over again. And he couldn't wait to get her back to his place, strip her of that beautiful gold dress and show her *exactly* how he felt about her.

They'd barely stepped over the threshold in Darius's darkened foyer when Audra grabbed him by the lapels of his tan Tom Ford suit and kissed him.

"Have I told you how dashing you looked tonight?" Audra glided her palms up his crisp, white dress shirt.

Then she slipped the jacket from his shoulders and onto a nearby chair in the foyer.

"You did, but I can't say I mind hearing it again." He trailed kisses down her neck. "Nor do I mind restating how stunning you look in that dress. Still, I'd much rather see you out of it."

He fumbled in the limited lighting to find the zipper that started beneath her arm and went down to her waist. He helped her shimmy out of it.

The cool air hit her skin as she stood in the foyer in the La Perla strapless bra and thong she'd purchased earlier that day.

Darius kissed her, his hands gliding down her back and squeezing her naked bottom.

The space between her thighs pulsed and throbbed, and her nipples tightened as the kiss grew more heated.

Audra unbuttoned his shirt and stripped him of it, then fumbled with the brown leather belt at his waist.

She glided down the zipper his hardened length strained against. He stepped out of the pants as they hit the floor.

Neither of them seemed to care about wrinkling the expensive garment.

She slipped her hand beneath the waistband of his underwear and wrapped her fingers around his heated flesh. She glided her thumb over its damp tip and pumped his length with her closed fist.

He gasped. His breathing became more shallow with each stroke.

As she brought him closer to the edge, his kiss became hungrier. Like he needed it as much as his next breath.

But then he grabbed her wrist and led her up the darkened stairs to his bedroom.

He laid her on the bed, but before he could kiss her again, she pressed a hand to his shoulder, stopping him.

"Dare, I've tried to convince myself that this was just a fling. That I could get involved with you again without it meaning anything." She swallowed hard, her pulse racing. "But that's a lie. The truth is I've fallen faster and harder for you now than I did then and…" Her voice wavered.

Feel whatever it is you feel. Don't try to avoid it.

"I love you, Darius."

It was too much too soon. But it was the truth. And she needed him to understand just how high the stakes were for her.

"Audra, baby…" He sighed quietly. "I love you, too. More than you know. But there are so many things we need to talk about. So many things I need to tell you."

"I know." She cut him off by pressing a thumb to his mouth, then gliding it across his lower lip. "But if it's all the same to you, I'd rather we didn't discuss them tonight. The last few days have been so perfect. Let's not ruin it." She pressed a soft kiss to his lips, then another.

They faced numerous challenges, if they wanted to make a real go at this relationship. Starting with their demanding careers, her family's objections and the logistics of him being in LA while she was in Dallas. And she wasn't ignoring any of that.

But for tonight, it was enough that he loved her, too. And that she'd been brave enough to admit that she loved him.

The rest they'd work out later.

In this moment, all she needed was for the man she loved to take her into his arms and make love to her as if nothing else in the world mattered but the two of them.

Twenty

Darius came out of his walk-in master closet, over-flowing with Thr3d sneakers and gear. It was Monday morning. But instead of returning to the office to follow up on the success of the runway show, he'd offered to pick his mother and Will up from the airport.

They'd seemed surprised that he'd offered. Which only exacerbated his guilt about how distant he'd been with them.

He glanced over at his bed where Audra was still sleeping. She'd forgotten to wear her usual silk head-scarf and her dark hair was spread out over the silk pillowcase.

The sheet was slung low over her bare back and one leg was tangled in the covers.

He chuckled. Audra was as wild a sleeper as she was a lover.

And he wouldn't change a thing about her.

He only hoped that after he told her the truth about why he'd come to Royal, she'd love him still.

He leaned down and pressed a kiss to the soft skin of her bare back and whispered in her ear. "I have some business to handle before I go into work this morning. But I'll call you as soon as I can."

She murmured something unintelligible, and he couldn't help smiling. He jotted down a note and left it on the table on her side of the bed.

"Darius, sweetie, it's so good to see you." His mother hugged him. Her face had lit up the moment she exited Los Angeles International Airport and saw him leaning against his black Range Rover.

"Hey, Mom." He hugged her back. "How was the trip?"

"Fantastic!" Will grinned, pulling their luggage behind him. "Just wait until I show you all of the pictures." He patted the camera around his neck. "How was your big fashion show?"

"Spectacular." Darius grabbed the luggage from his stepfather.

"Doesn't surprise us one bit." Will's blue eyes sparkled in the sunlight. He patted Darius's shoulder, then raked his fingers through the chin-length gray hair that had fallen into his face. "We've always believed in you, son."

Will had referred to him as *son* his entire life. But once Darius had learned Will wasn't his biological father, he'd cringed inside when the man referred to him that way. It had felt like just another part of their lie.

But it didn't feel that way now. Hearing Will call him *son* warmed his heart.

"Thanks," Darius said finally, unlocking the cargo gate and lifting it. The two of them put the luggage inside the truck.

On the drive to the home he'd purchased for them in Brentwood, he let the two of them chatter on about their three-week excursion. And he politely answered their questions about Thr3d's runway show.

Once he'd gotten them home and lugged their bags inside, he shoved his hand in his pocket and leaned against the wall. "I need to talk to you about something."

His mother nodded sadly as she and Will exchanged looks. "We thought as much."

"Let's have a seat." Will gestured toward the living room where Darius sat in the chair across from his parents. "All right, Darius. What's on your mind, son?"

He sucked in a deep breath. "I know who my biological father is."

"That can't be." His mother's eyes were filled with confusion. Will squeezed her hand and it seemed to calm her.

"I was summoned to Royal, Texas, by Miranda Dupree—Buckley Blackwood's ex-wife. He died a few months ago, and he charged her with finding me and telling me the truth about my paternity."

"That gutless bastard," his mother muttered. Tears filled her eyes and streamed down her cheeks. "All these years, he made us promise never to tell you and then he goes and pulls this stunt on his deathbed. If he wasn't already dead, I'd shoot him myself."

"Liberty, I know you're upset, but it's probably best

not to go saying you'd shoot the boy's father," Will said calmly.

"It was a cowardly move," his mother insisted, rising to her feet. "He could've had the decency to warn us he was going to pull this stunt. But as usual, he didn't give a damn about anyone but himself."

"That's not exactly true," Will, ever the voice of reason, countered. "He did provide for the boy. Made sure he was able to go to the best schools and had all of the necessities."

"The necessities a boy needs include the love, support and discipline of his father. Buckley Blackwood never provided any of that, Will. You did."

The truth of his mother's statement hit Darius hard. Will Pratt was a good man. He'd cared for Darius and loved him like he'd been his own flesh and blood. And all Darius had been able to see was that they'd lied to him.

He'd never asked himself why.

"Kellan Blackwood, my half brother, said that Buck may have tied some sort of nondisclosure to his financial support. Is that true?"

"You talked to one of Buck's sons?" His mother stopped pacing and stared at him in disbelief. "I mean, they were willing to talk to you? Despite…" Her words trailed off and she lowered her gaze.

"Despite the fact that you had an affair with their father while he was married to their mother?" He said the words without malice. "Yes. I was surprised about that, too."

His mother sat on the coffee table in front of him and pushed up her sleeves. "I didn't know he was married at the time. Not until afterward."

Darius raised a brow. "You honestly didn't know?"

"I swear to you, sweetheart. I didn't. I know I made a lot of bad choices back then, but believe me, even at my lowest, I thought far too highly of myself to willingly become anyone's side chick."

Now that did sound like his mother. She was in her late fifties and still turning heads.

"It wasn't until I told him I was pregnant that he admitted he was married. He offered..." She lowered her gaze to her clasped hands and sighed. "He knew that if his wife learned he'd fathered a child with someone else, she would've divorced him—and taken him to the cleaners. So when I was insistent that I wanted to raise you, he promised to take care of you financially as long as—"

"As long as you never revealed his identity to me."

"Or to anyone," she confirmed. "But then Will came into our lives when you were still quite young. He adored you, and when we got serious, I insisted on telling Will the truth." She reached back for her husband and he squeezed her hand. "But we've never told another soul...not even you, for fear he'd stop providing support or perhaps even take legal action."

Darius walked over to the window and stared out onto the manicured lawn. So many emotions weighed on his chest, he could barely breathe.

"Sweetheart, please say something." Liberty walked over to him.

"Like what, Ma? What am I supposed to say? That it sucks to know I was Buckley Blackwood's unwanted bastard child? That this explains why I felt like I never really belonged anywhere?"

"How can you say you were unwanted?" She cradled

his cheek. "I knew I was risking my career by taking time off to have a baby, especially as a single mother. But I didn't care, because from the moment I learned of you, you were mine, and I loved you more than anything else in the world. And think of Will." She dropped her hand from his cheek as they both turned to look at the man seated behind her. "Sometimes, I think he fell for you before he fell in love with me."

His mother and Will both chuckled.

"He had no obligation to you, Darius. Will *chose* to be your father. He even gave you his name. Does that sound like a man who didn't want you?"

"No." Darius sighed, rubbing his jaw. "It doesn't. And it's something I've been thinking about a lot these past few weeks. When you first told me Will wasn't my biological father, I was furious because a part of me believed that if you'd lied about Will being my dad, maybe you'd lied about my real father not wanting to be part of my life. And when you wouldn't even tell me who he was…" Darius shrugged. "I was bitter, angry and immature, and then I held a grudge against you both. Neither of you deserved that. I'm sorry. I realize now that you were both just trying to do right by me."

His mother hugged him tightly. Her tears wet his shirt. Will came over and hugged them both.

Suddenly, it felt as if he could breathe more easily. He couldn't regain the time they'd lost to his bitter grudge against his parents. The missed birthdays and anniversaries. But he could do right by them both going forward, just as they'd tried to do for him.

"Enough with the hug fest," Darius said, his own vision clouded. "There's a lot I need to catch the two of you up on."

Will grinned. "Let me put on a pot of coffee and you can tell us all about it."

Darius sat with his parents and explained that Buck had left all of his children out of the will, and that Sophie and Kellan had asked them to join them in contesting it. But that it would destroy his chances of working with Miranda's Goddess brand. Then he told them all about Audra and his time with her in Royal.

"I can't wait to meet this young lady." His mother beamed, sipping her coffee.

"And I can't wait for you to meet her," he said.

His phone rang. *Stasia.*

He excused himself to take the call.

Three international buyers wanted to place swimsuit orders if they could get an expedited delivery date.

Darius hadn't planned to go into the office today. Instead, he'd planned to return home and tell Audra everything right away.

But that conversation with Audra would have to wait a few hours longer.

"Sorry, Mom. Sorry, Wi—Dad, but we've got an emergency at the office. But I'll be in touch to make arrangements for you to meet Audra."

Will nodded, his eyes glossy. He'd obviously been moved by Darius calling him Dad for the first time since he'd learned the truth.

He hugged the man who'd taught him how to ride a bike. How to hit a baseball. How to be a responsible, loving man.

Then he went to the Range Rover and headed into the office. As soon as he'd resolved the issue at hand, he'd sit down with Audra and tell her the truth.

Twenty-One

Audra returned to Darius's house after an appointment with a real estate agent. The agent had showed her three available spaces. There was a newly vacant shop in Beverly Hills, a soon-to-be-available boutique at the Beverly Center and an office building in Pasadena that she could remodel to fit her specific needs. The Beverly Hills space had the right address for her upscale jewelry business, but the space in Pasadena was tempting because she could design it any way she wanted. And yes, maybe there was the additional lure of it being close to Darius's house.

She sat down to review her notes on each space, but her phone rang.

Cash.

He hadn't contacted her again since their chat at the Glass House in Royal. And since she'd threatened to never tell her mother anything again if she couldn't keep from blabbing her whereabouts to Cash, she doubted he was in Los Angeles looking for her.

This time, she wasn't going to ignore his call. Nor would she spare his feelings.

"Cash, why are you calling me?"

"You said we were still friends, right?" His voice sounded strange. "So I'm calling you as a friend."

She drew in a deep breath and sighed. "Well, you've caught me at a bad time. I'm working on something right now."

"In Los Angeles?"

Her cheeks flamed with heat. "So what, you're a stalker now, Cash?"

He laughed bitterly. "Hardly. I saw you in the fashion section of the local paper. I can't imagine your parents are too thrilled about you strutting down the runway in a bathing suit and making out with the designer at a rooftop bar."

"The photos are in the paper back in Dallas?" Now her face and neck really stung with heat.

It was a wonder her mother hadn't already called her in a panic with her usual speech about "behavior befitting a Covington."

"Thank you for the heads-up, Cash. I had no idea about the photos." Audra paced the floor. "I'd better call my mother before she hears it from someone else."

"Of all the women I've known, I always thought you were the one that never judged a man by the size of his bank account."

"I don't." Audra stopped her pacing and frowned. "You've known me most of my life, Cash. So why would you suddenly believe I've changed? I told you that Darius and I have known each other since grad school. Back when he had nothing but a dream and determination."

"So your newfound relationship with the guy has nothing to do with him being on the verge of inheriting millions?"

"What the hell are you talking about?"

"C'mon, Audra. Are you really going to tell me you had no idea that Darius Taylor-Pratt is the long-lost, secret heir of the late Buckley Blackwood? The half brother of your client, Sophie Blackwood?"

"No." Audra shook her head as she dropped into the closest chair, her knees suddenly giving way. "That's not possible. Darius or Sophie…one of them would've told me, if that were true."

"If you honestly didn't know, I guess neither of them is quite the friend you believed them to be," Cash said coolly.

"How sure are you about this?"

"DNA test sure." There was a bitter edge to his voice.

"And how would you know this?" The line went silent. "Cash, how do you know?" she demanded.

"I needed to know who this guy was. That he wasn't some user who'd only come back into your life because he needed something from you," he said. "I was only trying to protect you."

"By snooping into my life and the lives of my friends? I never asked you to do any of that."

"I thought I owed it to your parents to—"

"Oh, I get it. This isn't about me at all. If you can't become his son-in-law, you're going to try to impress my father by 'rescuing' me from a man you believe unworthy of James Covington's daughter."

"I resent the implication that I'm doing this for selfish reasons."

"I resent the fact that you're meddling in my business. I don't need or want your help. If you call me again, I'll tell my father, the police and the local newspapers that you've been stalking me and otherwise showing poor judgment by bribing hospital employees."

It was a guess, but it made sense. Who else could give Cash a peek at the results of a DNA test?

"Audra, I'm sorry for implying that you were after Darius for his family's fortune. But if he really didn't tell you why he came to town...well, it's obvious you can't trust anything this guy says. I don't want to see you get hurt."

"Call me again, Cash, and it'll be the end of your political career. You won't be able to get elected as dog catcher."

Audra ended the call and turned her phone off, dropping it onto the sofa beside her.

He lied to me again?

Her head felt light and there was a knot in her gut. She needed to talk to Darius. But she wanted to look him in the eyes when she did.

Audra wiped angrily at the tears that slid down her cheeks.

She needed a good long swim, a hot bath and a bottle of wine. Then, when Darius got home, the two of them were going to talk.

Darius returned to the house as quickly as he could. When he stepped inside, he was thrilled to see Audra, but she didn't look nearly as happy to see him. She sat at the kitchen island clutching a glass of white wine.

"Audra, sweetheart, is something wrong?" His heart suddenly beat harder.

"Is it true?"

"Is *what* true?"

She put the glass down, staring at him. "Is it true that you're Buckley Blackwood's son? That Sophie Blackwood is your younger sister? That the two of you conspired to get us back together? Was that why she hired me in the first place?"

"No! I mean, yes I am a Blackwood. But I swear to you, the first I learned of it was the day I landed in town. About an hour before you saw me at the diner. That's why I was there eating my comfort meal. I was devastated, confused... I didn't know what to think or if I could trust what I'd been told."

Her eyes were wet with tears. She wiped at them angrily, not allowing the tears to fall.

"So you lied to me. *Again.*" Her voice quivered.

The pain in her voice broke his heart. He'd let her down. *Again.*

"I didn't lie to you, Audra. I *did* go to Royal to do business with Miranda. But after I arrived, I learned that her real reason for bringing me there was to tell me that Buckley Blackwood, a man I'd never met, was my biological father."

"So you didn't lie about being a Blackwood the same way you didn't lie to me about your parents?" she asked incredulously, her arms folded.

"I deserved that." Darius ran a hand over his freshly shaved head and sighed. "But I swear to you, Audra, I planned to tell you everything just as soon as I could."

"When did you know for sure you were Blackwood's son?"

"I got the DNA test results the day we got paired up to volunteer at the TCC clubhouse."

"So you knew before we slept together." The pain in her eyes at the realization broke his heart. Because he'd hurt her again, even if he hadn't meant to.

"I did. But I couldn't say anything. Not until my parents got back in town, and I could talk to them face-to-face. I needed them to hear it from me first. I couldn't let them learn about it in the newspaper or on the cover of some magazine. They've been in Europe for the past three weeks."

She rolled her eyes. "Wow, that's convenient."

"It also happens to be true. I picked them up from the airport and told them this morning. I was going to rush back here to talk to you, but Stasia called me with a crisis at the office. As soon as we resolved it, I came right back here to tell you everything, I swear."

"I honestly don't know what to believe anymore, Darius." Audra hopped down from the bar stool. "Even if all that were true, it doesn't explain Sophie hiring me and pretending she didn't know my ex was her brother. Nor does it explain us ending up renting the houses next door to each other. There are just far too many coincidences here." She turned and walked toward the steps. "I may be gullible, but I'm not stupid."

"Audra!" He followed her up to his bedroom where she'd already pulled out her luggage and started to pack.

"I asked Sophie and Kellan not to tell anyone until I could tell my parents in person. That's why Sophie didn't tell you we were siblings."

"But she definitely knew. That's why she tried so hard to get us back together."

"Please don't be angry with Sophie. She was only

trying to respect my wishes and give me a chance to work all of this out."

Audra picked up the cutout peep-toe heels she'd been wearing when she'd showed up at his office and stuffed them into her suitcase.

"It's been killing me to keep this from you, but I had to protect my parents. I couldn't allow them to be blindsided by this the way they were by that article three years ago."

She continued to pack in silence, her cheeks and forehead flushed.

"Audra, sweetheart, you have to believe me." He lifted her chin gently, but she still wouldn't meet his gaze. "This is what I meant the other day when I said there was a lot we needed to talk about."

"So this is my fault because I didn't want to talk that night?" She pulled out of his grasp, suddenly indignant.

"No, of course not. How could you have known…" He rubbed the back of his neck, the realization suddenly dawning on him. "Wait…how *did* you know?"

"My ex called me this morning to accuse me of choosing you over him because you're a Blackwood." She held up a hand. "And yes, I'm pretty sure he did something either illegal or just plain shady as fuck to find out. But the point is, once again you've made a complete fool out of me, Darius. Because I believed in you. And I love you. But I don't know which is worse. That I'm not sure if I can trust you or that I *know* you don't trust me."

Her words hit him like a punch to the gut.

"Audra, it isn't that I didn't trust you. It just didn't feel right to tell anyone else until I'd talked to my parents. I owed them that much. I know you probably don't understand that—"

"No, I don't." Audra's voice trembled. She swiped a finger beneath her eye, then resumed her packing.

Darius sat on the edge of the bed they'd made love in, been so happy in, less than twelve hours ago.

"What can I do to prove that I'm telling you the absolute truth? I'll do anything, Audra." He grasped her hand. "Because I do love you. And there's no one in the world I'd rather be with."

She didn't look at him, but she didn't withdraw her hand from his grasp.

"I need some time to sort this all out. I'm sure you can understand that." She wouldn't look at him.

"Of course." He released her hand reluctantly. "But don't leave. You have client appointments booked all this week. You stay here. I'll go to a hotel, or maybe I'll crash at my parents' place."

"I'm not going to run you out of your own house."

"I want you to stay. Please. Just give me a few minutes to throw a bag together and I'll leave."

Darius grabbed the go-bag he kept in his closet and added a few more items. When he returned to the bedroom, Audra was still standing there, her arms wrapped around her middle.

"Thank you for giving me space." Her voice trembled, and she cast her gaze in the opposite direction. As if glancing at his face was too painful.

"For you, Audra? Anything." He hiked the bag on his shoulder. "I'll call in a few days. Call me, if you're ready to talk before then." He leaned in and kissed her cheek, then headed for the door.

She sank onto the bed, as if exhausted by the entire ordeal.

"Audra." He turned back to her briefly. "I really am sorry. I keep finding new and inventive ways to sabotage the thing I want most in the world. To be with you."

Darius got in the Range Rover and drove to his parents' house in Brentwood.

The thing he'd feared so, five years ago, had finally happened; Audra was rejecting him. And he deserved it.

Twenty-Two

Audra padded down the stairs in her bare feet. Given the circumstances, it was strange to be at Darius's house. But Darius had been adamant that she should stay. She was grateful for the offer, given her state of mind.

Audra called in a delivery order from her favorite Asian fusion restaurant in LA. While she was waiting, there was another call she needed to make.

The conversation had been stewing in her brain for the past eighteen hours.

She selected the number from her contacts list. A part of her hoped no one would answer.

"Hey, Audra! Are you still in LA?" a cheery voice greeted her.

"Yes, or didn't your brother tell you?" Audra tried not to sound snappy. After all, Sophie Blackwood was still a client.

"Kellan?" There was wariness in Sophie's voice. A sense that the jig was up.

"No." The word came out as a crisp, complete sentence. "Darius. Darius is your brother, isn't he?"

Sophie hesitated before answering. "Did Darius tell you that?"

"No. My ex did. Which made me feel pretty stupid since you both claim to be my friends." Audra paced the floor. "Darius gave me his excuses. Now I'd like to know why *you* didn't tell me that the ex I just happened to run into at Royal Diner was your long-lost brother."

Sophie sighed. "Darius didn't want anyone to know before he told his parents. And he didn't want his paternity to become a lurid headline that would steal the thunder from Thr3d's runway show. Besides, it wasn't my story to tell. So when Darius said he wasn't ready to divulge that information to the world...we respected his wishes," Sophie said contritely.

Audra could understand Darius's reasoning. It was considerate of him to deliver the news to his parents in person. A juicy tabloid headline about Blackwood's secret love child would definitely have overshadowed the positive press Thr3d was getting after their successful runway show. So at least their stories aligned.

But did he really equate her with the general public, not to be trusted with the information? The fact that he hadn't trusted her hurt even more.

"And Darius and I ending up in Royal simultaneously, renting houses next door to each other? That couldn't possibly be a coincidence." Audra plopped down in a chair in the family room off the kitchen. "Darius obviously put you up to this."

Sophie hesitated again. "Yes and no."

"What exactly does that mean?" Audra's patience was wearing thin.

"It means Darius had nothing to do with it."

"But you did?"

"Yes." Sophie sighed. "After we learned about Darius being our brother, I looked into him. I went through his social media accounts as far back as I could go. That led me to you. That's when I realized who you were and that the two of you were once together."

"So Darius didn't ask you to hire me?"

"No. I hadn't met him yet, and he still had no clue he was a Blackwood then. But when I learned his story, I felt bad about everything he'd been through. I wanted to do something for him. So I commissioned you to make our wedding rings and wedding party gifts. And I invited you to stay in town hoping—"

"That Darius and I would run into each other. God, Sophie. Life isn't like *The Parent Trap*. You can't trick people into getting back together."

"Well…it kind of worked, didn't it?"

"No, it most certainly did not." Audra's face got hot. She walked over to the patio door overlooking the pool. "At least, not now that I know you manufactured the entire thing. I do not like being manipulated. Putting us next door to each other and then telling me to use his swimming pool? That was incredibly shady."

"That's just the thing, I didn't realize he was in town until you told me. And I certainly had no idea Miranda had put him up at the house next door to the one you were renting. But when I learned that you two were staying next door to each other… Well, you really couldn't ask for a bigger sign, could you?"

"You just said you invited me to stay in town so Darius and I could meet. If you didn't arrange his arrival, how'd you plan to get the two of us together?" Audra asked, still dubious of Sophie's claims.

"I was going to reach out and ask him to spend a week in town leading up to my wedding. I figured you'd still be here, too. I planned to place you two together at the pre-wedding festivities."

Audra sank her teeth into her lower lip, trying to decide whether or not to believe her.

"And all that talk about us being friends…that was part of your plan, too?" she asked finally.

"No, of course not. I genuinely like you, Audra. It didn't take long for me to see why my brother adores you."

"Did Darius talk to you about me?"

"Never. But he didn't need to. Anyone who's seen you two together can see just how much he adores you and how into him you are. When you said you were going to LA for his show, I was thrilled. And then when I saw that photo in the paper of you two kissing—"

"You saw it, too?"

"I did." There was a giddy grin in Sophie's voice. "And I couldn't have been happier for both of you."

Audra sighed. "Thank you for your honesty, Sophie. I'll see you back in Royal in a few days. I have a few more things to handle here in LA."

"So you'll still be at the wedding?" The joy in Sophie's voice was evident.

"A promise is a promise," Audra muttered. "I might not appreciate your matchmaking scheme, but I don't doubt your heart was in the right place. Speaking of the wedding, will everything be ready at the clubhouse in time?"

"Everything is ready, but I had another idea. My mom and dad are gone, but I thought that if I could have the wedding at Blackwood Hollow, then at least I'd have the memories of my parents surrounding me. Sounds corny, right?"

"No, Sophie. That sounds lovely."

"I've been trying to get up the nerve to ask Miranda, since she owns the estate now."

"Nigel knows her pretty well, doesn't he? If he thinks she'd be open to the idea, then you should at least try. Give Miranda a chance. Maybe she'll surprise you."

The doorbell rang, and Audra said her goodbyes. When she opened the door, a scruffy older man with chin-length gray hair and sparkling blue eyes stood at the door, holding her delivery bag. Something about him looked incredibly familiar, though she couldn't place him.

Not surprising. Half of the people in LA were current, former or aspiring actors.

She held up the tip, taking the bag from him.

The man released the bag but waved off the tip. He jerked a thumb over his shoulder. "I already tipped the guy, though not nearly as generously as you were going to," he said.

"If you're not the delivery guy…" Audra took a few steps back, her eyes scanning the space for anything she could use as a weapon. "Who the hell are you?"

"Guess that wasn't the best introduction." He chuckled good-naturedly and extended his hand. "Hello, Audra. I'm William Pratt, Darius's stepfather."

Now she remembered where she'd seen the man's face. There were photos of Darius's mother and stepfather in his guestroom and one in his office.

She shook the man's hand. "Good to meet you, Mr. Pratt. But if you know who I am, then you probably know Darius isn't here and why. So how can I help you?"

"May I come in?" The two men might not be related by blood, but it was obvious where Darius had gotten his charm.

She let him in, taking the food to the kitchen and washing her hands. She set out two place settings. "I hope you like Asian fusion because I got carried away and ordered too much."

"I'll try anything once." He shrugged.

Audra divided the food on their plates, giving him a small portion to sample. She climbed onto a stool and opened her chopsticks.

"So why was it that you wanted to see me, Mr. Pratt?"

"Call me, Will, please." He studied the small portions of braised pork, thinly sliced, marinated Angus beef and ground chicken as if he wasn't sure which would be the least offensive to his taste buds.

"May I suggest you start with the marinated beef?" She held back a grin. "It's particularly good with the rice."

He nodded his thanks and tried a bite. Then he smiled. "Not bad."

"Did Darius send you here?" She picked up some of the braised pork with her chopsticks.

"No, and I'll likely have quite a bit of explaining to do once he finds out." The man's eyes crinkled with a small smile. "But he was just so down about what happened between you. I just couldn't sit by and not do anything. Figured talking to you was at least worth a try."

Audra studied the man as he tried the braised pork. He seemed genuine, and he obviously cared very much for Darius.

She put her chopsticks down and sat up tall in her seat as she faced the man.

"All right, Mr. Pratt—"

"Will."

"All right, Will. What is it that you came to say in Darius's defense?"

The man put his fork down and wiped his mouth and scraggly beard with one of the white napkins. He turned toward her.

"I came to remind you of what you probably already know. Darius has made some mistakes, but he's a good man."

"How can you say that when he walked away from you two, just like he walked away from me back in grad school?"

"Even when he was angry with his mother and me, he still took care of us. Bought us a home the moment he could afford to. Sends us money every month to supplement our incomes. And as for you, Audra, I suspect he never stopped thinking of you. Never stopped rehashing the horrible mistake he made in walking away from you because he was afraid you'd eventually turn your back on him."

"I would never have done that."

"I think he knows that now," the man said kindly.

"He still obviously doesn't trust me, or he wouldn't have believed that I'd leak the info to the media." It hurt her just to say the words.

"I don't suspect he believed that of you at all. But it's a sensitive subject, and I think he felt guilty about talking to anyone about it while his mother and I were still in the dark. I suspect that had a lot to do with the guilt he felt over that magazine article that came out a few years ago."

"You're a thoughtful man, Will Pratt. Darius is lucky to have you as a father."

"Thank you, Audra." A wide grin spread across the man's face. "Before I go, there's one more thing I want you to know."

"Yes?" She picked up her chopsticks again.

"My son loves you very much. I know he's made some flubs where we're both concerned. But the rejection and betrayal he felt when he learned I wasn't his biological father...it hit him hard and he's been struggling ever since. If you can find it in your heart to give him another chance, I know he's worth it."

Will thanked her for the meal and left.

Audra closed the door behind him and sighed.

She loved Darius. But that wasn't enough if he didn't trust her and if she couldn't trust him.

One thing she realized for sure; she needed the time and space to figure this out for herself. And she couldn't do that here, in the house where everything reminded her of Darius. After her meal, Audra rescheduled her remaining client meetings and booked herself a flight for Dallas.

She needed the comfort of home.

Twenty-Three

Darius stared at the note in his hand, studying the perfect penmanship. Aesthetically, it was beautiful. Almost worthy of being framed and hung on the wall. But its contents were devastating.

Audra had returned to Dallas, declaring that she needed the time and space to think. She'd asked him to allow her that.

So that was what he was doing. It'd been a week since she'd left that note on his nightstand after sending him a text message to say he could come back to his house because she was already on a plane heading home.

Stasia walked into his office and he dropped the note, shifting a blue file folder on top of it.

Her attention went directly to the corner of the note, which peeked out from beneath the file folder.

He obviously wasn't fooling her.

She closed the door behind her and sank into one of the chairs on the opposite side of his desk. "I'm really sorry, Darius. Audra obviously means a lot to you."

"Thanks," he muttered, not looking up. He'd given Stasia the basics on what had happened between him and Audra when she'd persisted in asking.

Mostly so she'd stop. And so she'd understand if he was a bit short with everyone.

"Look, I know she asked for space, and I'm glad you're respecting her request. But you should let her know how deeply you care for her. Before she ends up hooking up with some other guy, like her shady ex, the tattler. What if they make a connection? Are you gonna wait until she's walking up to the altar with this guy before you speak up? Or maybe you plan to wait until her first baby shower or—"

"All right, Stasia." He held up a hand.

It tore a hole in his heart to think of Audra getting with some other guy, like that low-life, politician ex who'd obviously used sleazy tactics to delve into his past.

"You've made your point. But if she doesn't want to talk to me, what am I supposed to do? I don't know if you've heard the news, but creepy dudes who can't take no for an answer are definitely out for the foreseeable future. So I don't want to be that guy."

"There is a delicate line to walk," she acknowledged. "So I'm certainly not encouraging you to harass her like her jerk ex-boyfriend. But you can't just sit here and do nothing. Send her an email. Leave a voice message. Send her something through snail mail. Hell, hire a skywriter or the Goodyear blimp, if you have to. Just don't let this phenomenal, brilliant, amazing woman go without a fight. I definitely wouldn't. You don't think I snagged a woman as gorgeous as May by sitting up in my office and wallowing in my feelings for a week, do you?"

"I thought May asked you out." He folded his arms.

"Totally not the point." She leveled a finger at him.

"What is the point, Stasia?" He shuffled some papers, busily.

She got up from her chair, taking the hint. "The point is don't compound your past mistakes with an even bigger one. If you let Audra walk away again, we both know you'll never forgive yourself." She frowned, fiddling with one of the two cotton candy–colored braids her hair was divided into. "Oh, and Miranda Dupree called before you arrived. She asked if you'll be in Royal again soon because she has some designs she'd like to show you. She said no tricks this time. She emailed a few preliminary sketches to prove it. I forwarded them to you."

"Do me a favor, Stas. Get Miranda on the phone. Before I agree to anything, she and I need to talk, so that we're not wasting each other's time."

"I'll buzz you as soon as I get her on the line." Anastasia left his office and closed the door, putting Miranda through a minute later.

"Didn't trust me not to pull any more shenanigans?" Miranda asked, teasingly. "The invitation is straightforward this time. I already sent proof."

"Thank you for that," Darius said. "But that isn't why I called. I've decided that if Sophie and Kellan move forward with contesting the estate, I'm going to join them. So if that's a deal-breaker for you—"

"I honestly think that Buck would be happy to know

that the three of you banded together." There was a hint of laughter in her voice. "And no, I'm not offended by your decision. I would do the same thing in your place. As for this, it's business. I was already on board with this collaboration, but after seeing your fall collection, especially the rollout of the swimwear, I have no doubt that Thr3d is who we want to partner with on this project."

He breathed out a quiet sigh of relief.

"Thank you for understanding my position, Miranda. I have a few things to wrap up here in LA, but I can be back in Royal by the day after tomorrow. Let's say we'll meet on Thursday at 1 p.m.?"

Miranda agreed to the time and he forwarded the info to Stasia, advising her that he'd be working from his satellite office in Royal for the next week or so.

First, he'd settle this deal with Goddess. Then, if he hadn't heard from Audra, he'd take Stasia's advice, even if he had to send his message via carrier pigeon.

"This preliminary meeting has gone far better than I expected." Miranda scanned the design options Darius had brought as part of Thr3d's collaboration proposal. "I don't know how I'm going to narrow it down to just fifteen pieces."

"I'm glad you're pleased." Darius sat in the same chair he'd occupied the first day he'd come to Royal. The day he'd discovered that he was Buckley Blackwood's son. "I'm particularly glad that you like our interpretation of your preliminary sketches."

"They're amazing." Miranda picked up one of the legging tracksuit designs his team had reimagined. "I honestly couldn't be more thrilled. So if Thr3d is ready to move forward on this, Goddess is, too. We'll let the lawyers hash out the details of the contract."

Darius agreed and they exchanged their lawyers' business cards.

Miranda picked up the house phone and took a call. She hung up the phone after very few words.

"We have a guest I think you'll be interested in seeing. Your sister, Sophie."

"How did she know I was in town?" he asked.

"She probably doesn't. She's here to see me." Miranda sat on the front edge of the desk.

"Darius, hey." Sophie stepped into the office and gave him a big smile. She hugged him warmly before turning to her former stepmother. "Miranda, thank you for seeing me on such short notice."

"We're all done, so I'll head out and give you two privacy," Darius said.

"Actually, I'd prefer that you stay." Sophie leaned in and whispered, "I could use the moral support."

"Sure." He gave her an encouraging smile and returned to his seat. Sophie sat beside him.

"As you know, Miranda, I'm getting married soon. Lately, I've been thinking that I'd really like to have the wedding here at Blackwood Hollow. Both of my parents are gone, but if we could have the wedding here, at least I'll be surrounded by the happy memories I have of them. I realize this is very last minute, and it would be an inconvenience for you, but if—"

"Of course you can have the wedding here, Sophie," Miranda interrupted Sophie's nervous babbling. "I think that's a wonderful idea. Your father would've loved it."

Sophie looked shocked. "Oh, well…thank you, Miranda. That means a lot to Nigel and me. I know it'll mean a lot to Kellan and Vaughn, too."

"My pleasure. Please let me know if I can help with the arrangements in any way." Miranda walked around the desk and sat behind it again.

Sophie and Darius stood and turned to leave, but then Sophie turned back, reluctantly.

"One more thing."

"Yes?" Miranda smiled at her brightly.

"You're welcome to attend."

"Oh. Well, thank you, Sophie." Miranda tucked strands of her fiery red hair behind one ear. Her blue eyes suddenly looked misty. "I'd like that very much."

As Sophie and Darius headed to their cars, Darius nudged her with his elbow. "That wasn't so difficult, now, was it?"

"Thankfully." She sighed. "Lately, I seem to muck up even the simplest things. You and Audra found your way to each other with minimal interference from me. And then she figured out that I'd meddled in your affairs and…" Sophie shook her head and sighed. "Darius, I'm so sorry about making trouble between you and Audra. I messed everything up."

Darius hugged his sister. "It's not your fault, Soph. It's mine. And I have to find a way to fix this."

"You two are perfect for each other. I hope you can work things out."

"Me, too." He squeezed her shoulder, then headed toward his rental.

"Wait, Darius, how long will you be in town?"

"A week, maybe."

"Perfect. I'd like to give you an official welcome celebration. Maybe this Saturday at seven at my place?"

He was going to decline. But Sophie was being thoughtful and welcoming. He should embrace it.

Wasn't that what he'd always wanted?

"Sounds great, Sophie. I'll see you then."

"And you're welcome to bring along a plus-one." A broad smile animated her brown eyes.

Darius got inside his rental SUV and sucked in a deep breath.

It'd been a good day so far. Miranda was moving forward with their deal and had granted Sophie's wedding venue request. Maybe this was the day to reach out to Audra.

Darius returned to his rental home and stood at the window overlooking the pool. He dialed Audra's number. It went immediately to voice mail.

"Hey, Audra. I realize you asked for time and space, and I respect that. But I wanted to tell you again how sorry I am about the mistakes I made then and now." His heart pounded in his chest, and his throat suddenly felt dry. "I'm standing in the rental house in Royal, looking at the pool, thinking of the first day I saw you there. I couldn't believe I'd been given a second chance to make things right with you. And I still managed to screw things up."

Darius swallowed hard, wondering how much longer he had before the call would cut off.

Quit babbling, and just say it.

"I miss you, Audra. And I love you. More than anything. I can't imagine the rest of my life without you in it."

His chest felt tight and it was harder to breathe. He was going to hang up. But there was something else he needed to say.

"One more thing. Sophie's having a little get-together this Saturday at seven to officially welcome me to town and to the family. I understand if you'd rather not attend, but nothing would make me happier than if you could be there. Take care of yourself, Audra."

Darius set the phone on the counter, hoping she'd call him right away. But she didn't. Not that day or the next.

He'd blown it with Audra, and Stasia was right. For that, he'd never forgive himself.

Twenty-Four

Audra inhaled a deep breath and stepped out of her car. She'd been to Sophie and Nigel's place several times. But this trip was notably different.

Her belly did flips, and her legs felt like Jell-O. She couldn't remember the last time she'd been this nervous.

When she stepped inside, Tessa's face was the first one she recognized.

"Audra, I didn't realize you were in town." Tessa leaned in and hugged her. "Everyone will be thrilled to see you."

"I hope so." Audra forced a smile.

"I know so." Tessa squeezed her hand and grabbed a glass of champagne from a passing tray. She handed the flute to Audra, as if she sensed that she needed it.

She thanked Tessa and gulped some of the bubbly liquid. It tickled her nose.

"Audra! It's great to see you." Lulu Shepard leaned in and surprised Audra with a hug.

The woman was practically beaming as Kace wrapped his arm around her waist, tucking her close to his side.

Look who's not being so mysterious about his feelings anymore.

Kace smiled at her warmly. "Good to have you back in Royal, Audra."

He quickly returned his attention to Lulu. A giddy, love-struck gaze softened his usually serious expression.

They were an adorable couple, and Audra was truly happy for them.

The clinking of a spoon against a glass drew the crowd's attention to where the Blackwood family stood with Darius at the center.

"Vaughn sends his apologies that he couldn't be here with us," Kellan said, a glass of champagne in his hand. "But for everyone who doesn't know, Darius Taylor-Pratt is our brother. Sophie, Nigel, Irina and I just wanted to formally introduce him to you as such and say welcome to our crazy family." Kellan slipped an arm around the waist of his expectant bride. With her strawberry blond hair, dark green eyes and porcelain features, Irina practically glowed.

"To Darius." Kellan held up his glass and everyone followed suit, clinking their glasses with their neighbors and then sipping their champagne.

Audra strained her neck to see Darius through the house full of people, most of whom she recognized from volunteering at the TCC clubhouse. He seemed reluctant to have all of the attention on himself, as he had been during the end of Thr3d's runway show. But he also seemed quietly content to be accepted by this new community and by the siblings he'd never known.

"Thank you, Kellan, Sophie, Nigel and Irina for welcoming me to the Blackwood family." Darius smiled affectionately at his siblings and their partners. "You've been nothing but supportive. Words simply can't convey just how much I appreciate you."

Darius turned his attention to the crowd gathered in front of him. "Thank you all for coming tonight, and for your warm welcome and the sense of community you've extended to me. I look forward to spending a lot more time here in Royal and getting to know you all." He nodded his thanks in response to the enthusiastic applause.

Darius's eyes scanned the space. His eyes lit up when they met hers.

Her belly fluttered and her pulse raced. She offered a small, inconspicuous wave, and her mouth quirked in an involuntary smile.

His smile widened and he whispered something to Sophie, who cast a glance in her direction and pressed a hand to her chest. She waved at Audra, her eyes dancing with joy.

Darius made a beeline through the crowd. "Audra, I'm so glad you're here." He hugged her as if he had no intentions of letting her go. "When you didn't respond to my message—"

"I missed you, too," Audra blurted the words out. She'd listened to the voice message from Darius at least a dozen times. Reluctantly, she pulled back from his embrace so she could meet his gaze. "I know this isn't the time or place, but we need to talk."

Darius led Audra by the hand down a dimly lit hall and into Sophie's office. He switched on the light. And they settled onto the small sofa.

He turned his body toward hers and held her hands in his. "Okay, Audra, I'm ready to hear whatever it is you came to say."

"But this party is for you. Won't Sophie and the others be looking for you?"

"Nothing matters more to me right now than you. My sister will understand." His expression was a mixture of hope and apprehension. "So first, let me assure you that everything I said in that voice mail, I meant. I love you, Audra." He pressed a light kiss to the back of her hand. "I'm sorry I couldn't tell you everything from the start. I really wanted to."

"I believe you." She squeezed his hand. "I understand why you felt you couldn't tell me in the beginning. But I do wish you'd told me before LA."

"So do I. This past week without you…" There was pain in his voice. "I was afraid I'd lost you forever. I've never been more miserable in my life."

"Me, too." She swallowed hard and freed one hand to tuck her hair behind her ear. "I want this to work, Darius. I really do. But I need to know you trust me. *Fully.* The same way you'd want me to trust you. We're either full partners in this relationship or there isn't one."

"I do trust you, Audra. You're the only woman I want in my life." Darius kissed her palm and her belly fluttered. "Forgive me?"

"Yes," she whispered the word as he planted a soft kiss on her wrist and then trailed a string of them up her arm. She pulled away from him and tried to clear her head. Darius needed to understand that she meant what she was about to say. She poked a finger in his chest. "But no more secrets."

"Promise." He nodded solemnly, then captured her mouth in a kiss that was sweet and tentative. But it quickly became intense. Hungry and feverish. Filled with longing, want and desperation.

Audra ached to crawl onto his lap and straddle him, deepening their kiss. But they were likely already the talk of the party. She pressed the heel of her hand against his chest, tearing her mouth from his.

"We'd better get back out there before your little sister comes looking for us." She kissed him once more before climbing to her feet. "But there's one more thing. My parents will be in LA in a few weeks, and I want them to meet you."

He stood, too, looping his arms around her waist. "And what if they don't approve?"

She shrugged. "I *want* them to like you. But I don't *need* them to. Who I love is my choice, not theirs."

He nodded, one edge of his mouth curled with satisfaction at her response. "I'd be honored to meet them," he said. "And you've already met my dad. So my mom's a little jealous. She insisted that I bring you by for dinner the next time you're in LA."

"I can't wait to meet her." Audra grinned.

"We're going straight to the meet-the-parents stage." Darius smiled broadly. "Guess that means this is serious."

"I've never been more serious about anything in my life." The truth of the admission was both terrifying and thrilling.

"Good." He grinned. "I know we still have to work

out the logistics. But I'm more than willing to compromise."

"Speaking of logistics…there's something I haven't had a chance to tell you. I leased a shop on Rodeo Drive while I was in Los Angeles." She giggled in response to his look of disbelief. "It was the right decision for my brand. A move I've been contemplating for at least two years. But the bonus is that there's this amazing guy I've fallen for, and he just happens to live in LA."

"Congratulations, Audra. That's fantastic news." Darius hugged her again. "But this won't be a one-sided compromise. I'll be spending a lot more time here in Texas, getting to know the family I've inherited and reacquainting myself with the woman I haven't been able to get out of my head for the past five years."

She beamed, her heart bursting with love and a deep sense of joy. Tears clouded her vision.

"One more thing, beautiful." He brushed the dampness from her cheek with his thumb. "I miss everything about us. Talking to you all night. Falling asleep with you in my arms. Your face being the first one I see each morning. Our early breakfasts and late dinners together. Bubble bath therapy and the tranquility of watching you swim laps in my pool."

The words coming from Darius's mouth were rushed. He paused, inhaling deeply.

"I know we're both busy trying to build empires—" his lips curved in a nervous smile "—but I want to spend every available moment with you. So…what I'm trying to say is… I love you, Audra, and I'd love it if you'd move in with me."

"In LA?" She'd hoped he'd offer but hadn't wanted to push.

"And here in Royal. Or maybe your place in Dallas?" He nuzzled her cheek. "No pressure, if you feel we're moving too fast."

"No, we're not moving too fast." Audra shook her head, without an ounce of doubt. "We're moving five years too slow. And I can't wait to make up for lost time." Her mouth stretched in a playful grin. "Besides, I *really* like that pool."

Darius laughed, the tension in his expression easing. His eyes were filled with emotion as he leaned in and pressed his warm, open mouth to hers and tunneled his fingers into her hair as he angled her face. Audra tipped her head back and clutched his shirt, eager for more of his kiss.

So maybe the party would have to wait a while longer.

* * * * *

Don't miss a single installment of
Texas Cattleman's Club: Inheritance

Tempting the Texan *by*
USA TODAY *bestselling author*
Maureen Child

Rich, Rugged Rancher *by Joss Wood*
Available January 2020

From Boardroom to Bedroom *by*
USA TODAY *bestselling author*
Jules Bennett

Secret Heir Seduction *by Reese Ryan*

Too Texan to Tame *by Janice Maynard*
Available April 2020

Her Texas Renegade *by*
USA TODAY *bestselling author*
Joanne Rock
Available May 2020

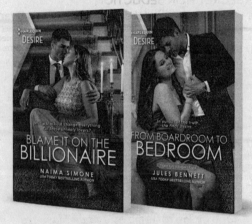

"So, as you can see, my father will stop at nothing to get what he
wants. He doesn't care who he hurts or maligns in the process. I
refuse to let your family become involved."

A frown settled on his face. "That's not your decision to make."

"What do you mean it's not my decision to make?"

"The Steeles can take care of ourselves."

"But you don't know my father."

"Wrong. Your father doesn't know us."

Mercury wondered if anyone had ever told Sloan how cute
she looked when she became angry. How her brows slashed
together over her forehead and how the pupils of her eyes became
a turbulent dark gray. Then there was the way her chin lifted and
her lips formed into a decadent pout. Observing her lips made him
remember their taste and how the memory had kept him up most
of the night.

"I don't need you to take care of me."

Her words were snapped out in a vicious tone. He drew in a
deep breath. He didn't need this. Especially from her and definitely
not this morning. He'd forgotten to cancel his date last night with

Raquel and she had called first thing this morning letting him know she hadn't appreciated it. It had put him in a bad mood, but, unfortunately, Raquel was the least of his worries.

"You don't?" he asked, trying to maintain a calm voice when more than anything he wanted to snap back. "Was it not my stolen car you were driving?"

"Yes, but—"

"Were you not with me when you discovered you were being evicted?" he quickly asked, determined not to let her get a word in, other than the one he wanted to hear.

"Yes, but—"

"Did I not take you to my parents' home? Did you not spend the night there?"

Her frown deepened. "Has anyone ever told you how rude you are? You're cutting me off deliberately, Mercury."

"Just answer, please."

She didn't say anything and then she lifted her chin a little higher, letting him know just how upset she was when she said, "Yes, but that doesn't give you the right to think you can control me."

Control her? Was that what she thought? Was that what her rotten attitude was about? Well, she could certainly wipe that notion from her mind. He bedded women, not controlled them.

"Let me assure you, Sloan Donahue, controlling you is the last thing I want to do to you." There was no need to tell her that what he wouldn't mind doing was kissing some sense into her again.

Don't miss what happens next in
Seduced by a Steele
by Brenda Jackson, part of her Forged of Steele series!

Available April 2020 wherever
Harlequin Desire books and ebooks are sold.

Harlequin.com

SPECIAL EXCERPT FROM

HQN

When India Robidoux needs help with her brother's high-profile political campaign, she has no choice but to face the one man she's been running away from for years—Travis, her sister's ex-husband. One hot summer night when Travis was still free, they celebrated her birthday with whiskey and an unforgettable kiss. The memory is as strong as ever—and so are the feelings she's tried so hard to forget...

Read on for a sneak peek of
Forbidden Promises by Synithia Williams

"We need everyone else in the family to demonstrate that family and friendships are still strong despite the divorce. I'm pairing Travis up with Byron and India."

India's jaw dropped. Everyone turned to her. Everyone except Elaina, who stood even more rigid next to the window.

"Me? Why me?" The words came out in a weird croak and she cleared her throat.

"Because you make sense," Roy explained.

Travis crossed the room to the food. India quickly stepped out of his way. Her hip bumped the table, rattling the platters set on the surface. Travis raised an eyebrow. She forced herself to relax and nod congenially. She wasn't supposed to react when he was near. They were cool now. They'd cleared the air. Deemed what had happened years ago a mistake. She couldn't run and hide when he came near.

She focused on Roy. "What do I have to do?"

"There will be a few times when we'll need family members to campaign for Byron if he can't be there personally. We've got a lot of ground to cover, and if we can show a united front, I'd recommend having at least two family members together in those cases. I'll partner you with Travis for those appearances. The two of you can play up how great he is as a brother and friend."

Roy made it all sound so easy. Sure, everything seemed simple to everyone else. They didn't realize the easy friendship she'd once shared with Travis was gone. No one knew she could barely look at him without thinking about how she'd loved him. How she'd dreamed about his kiss even after he'd married Elaina. Fought to forget the feel of his hands on her body as she'd stood next to her sister at their wedding.

"Now that that's settled," Roy said, obviously taking India's silence as agreement, "we can get to the next point."

"Are you okay with spending time with me?" Travis asked in a low voice.

India's heart did a triple beat. He'd slid close to her as Roy moved on. His proximity was like an electric current vibrating against her skin.

"Of course," she said quickly. "Why wouldn't I be?"

"You wouldn't be the only person not wanting my company lately."

The disappointment in his voice made her look up. He wasn't looking at her. He frowned at the floor. His lips were pressed into a tight line. She wanted to reach out and touch him. To attempt to erase the sadness from his features. "I'll always want your company."

His head snapped up and he studied her face. She really shouldn't have said that. The words were too close to how she really felt.

"We'll need to pick out a suitable fiancée for him."

Roy's voice and the randomness of his words broke India from the captivating hold of Travis's eyes. She tuned back into the conversation. "Fiancée? Who needs a fiancée?"

Byron chuckled and placed a hand on his chest. "I do."

India looked from her father to Byron. Were they serious? "You didn't mention you were getting married."

Byron shrugged as if not mentioning a possible fiancée wasn't a huge deal. "I didn't decide to ask her until recently. We've been dating for a few months."

Dating for a few months? Wasn't he the same guy Travis had teased about three women calling him just yesterday? Her brother was a ladies' man, but he wasn't a dog. He wouldn't be considering marriage to someone if he still had multiple women calling his phone. Would he? Had he changed that much while she'd been gone?

She spun toward Travis. "You aren't letting him do this, are you?" She pointed over her shoulder at her brother.

Travis stilled with a chocolate croissant halfway to his mouth. "Do what?"

She stepped closer and lowered her voice. "Marry this Yolanda person. Who is she? Are they really dating?"

Travis sighed. "They've gone back and forth for a while."

Which really meant that her brother had been sleeping with her for a few months, but there was no commitment. Her hands balled into fists. She couldn't believe this!

"Don't spout off the campaign bullshit with me," she said in a low voice that wouldn't carry to her plotting relatives still in the room. "Not with me. This is a campaign maneuver."

"Roy has a point." Travis said the words slowly, as if he couldn't believe he was agreeing with Roy. "Your brother can't be a senator if he's out there picking up women in bars. He's got to settle down. Yolanda is who he chose."

"Did he choose her?" She wouldn't doubt that Roy, or their dad, picked the perfect woman for him.

"He said he chose her."

"Do you believe him?"

Travis glanced at the group huddled together. "I want to believe him. Giving up what you want for an unhappy marriage isn't worth the price of a senate seat." He turned a heavy gaze on her. "Not when it ruins a true chance at happiness."

India leaned back. She was stunned into silence. Her throat was dry and her stomach fell to her feet. The regret in his eyes created a deep ache in her chest. Had he given up something for an unhappy marriage? Before the words could spill from her lips, he took a bite of the croissant and strolled over to join the strategizing team, leaving India with another unanswered question to taunt her at night.

Don't miss what happens next in
Forbidden Promises by Synithia Williams!
Available February 2020 wherever
HQN books and ebooks are sold.

HQNBooks.com

PHSWEXP0320